Claudia and the Lighthouse Ghost

Caryn Pearson

Other books by
Ann M. Martin

Leo The Magnificat
Rachel Parker, Kindergarten Show-off
Eleven Kids, One Summer
Ma and Pa Dracula
Yours Turly, Shirley
Ten Kids, No Pets
With You and Without You
Me and Katie (the Pest)
Stage Fright
Inside Out
Bummer Summer

THE KIDS IN MS. COLMAN'S CLASS series
BABY-SITTERS LITTLE SISTER series
THE BABY-SITTERS CLUB mysteries
THE BABY-SITTERS CLUB series

THE BABY-SITTERS CLUB

Claudia and the Lighthouse Ghost
Ann M. Martin

AN
APPLE
PAPERBACK

SCHOLASTIC INC.
New York Toronto London Auckland Sydney

Cover art by Hodges Soileau

ISBN 0-590-69175-9

12 11 10 9 8 7 6 5 4 3 2 1   6 7 8 9/9 0 1/0

Printed in the U.S.A.   40

First Scholastic printing, December 1996

The author gratefully acknowledges
Peter Lerangis
for his help in
preparing this manuscript.

Claudia and the Lighthouse Ghost

CHAPTER 1

"H o-o-o-neee, I'm ho-o-ome!" I called out.

It was a perfect imitation of Ricky Ricardo. Well, as perfect as a thirteen-year-old girl can make it. I even impressed myself.

I closed the front door behind me and waited for the reaction.

My friend Abby Stevenson and I had been working on a routine from an *I Love Lucy* re-run. We'd just been baby-sitting for the seven Barrett/DeWitt kids that afternoon, and we'd had them in hysterics.

I could hear my parents upstairs. (Lucky me. My mom is sometimes back from work at five o'clock on Fridays, but Dad only rarely makes it home early.) Their voices were muffled, so I figured they were in their bedroom.

Time for the Ricky laugh. I closed up my throat and made a sound like a seal's bark: "HA! HA! HA! HA!" You would have thought Desi Arnaz was there in the Kishi living room.

Click. I heard my parents' door open. "Hello, Claudia Lynn," my mom called out.

My older sister, Janine, appeared at the top of the stairs, wearing headphones. "Did you bring a dog home?" she asked.

"Nope," I said. "It's just me. Can you tell who I was imitat — ?"

"Then will you please stop yapping?" Janine barged on. "I'm listening to my astrophysics lecture."

Uh-huh. Right.

How many kids do you know with high-school-age sisters who take astrophysics? I'll bet you can count them on the fingers of one elbow.

It's not easy living with a genius. My sister takes courses at a local college, for fun. I happen to think her idea of fun is seriously twisted.

Now, I love Janine dearly, but we do not have a lot in common. For one thing, when teachers see her IQ score, they go weak in the knees.

Actually, they go weak in the knees when they see mine, too. But for a different reason.

I wouldn't know astrophysics from Astro-Turf. And I couldn't begin to spell either one of them. Mention history and I start to droop. I used to think algebra was a type of lingerie.

Which is why I, at age thirteen, am the oldest seventh-grader at Stoneybrook Middle School in Stoneybrook, Connecticut. Yes, I should be in eighth grade, but I was sent back.

My parents, needless to say, were not pleased about that. (I wasn't too thrilled either.) They're pretty brainy themselves. Dad's an investment banker and Mom's a librarian. They both believe in High Achievement and Proper Education. Of course, they worship Janine.

Me they tolerate. They try very hard to see me for who I really am. But I do wish they'd stop wearing masks when we're together in public.

Just kidding.

What am I really like? I'm Japanese-American, for starters. Actually, you could tell a lot about me from the way I looked that day: I was wearing a white high-collared dentist's shirt and a loose-fitting Chinese silk jacket, cinched at the waist by a bright-orange scarf, over tight black flared pants. My hair was gathered on top of my head with an orange bandanna.

I know, you think I'm demented. But trust me, it looked great. Anyone can copy an outfit from a model in *Seventeen*, but it takes talent to make a funky cool outfit out of stuff from thrift stores and yard sales.

That's how I look at life — creating something wild and beautiful from unexpected sources.

Maybe that's why I don't do well in school. In math, for instance, I love to make interesting shapes out of the numbers and symbols. I kind of lose track of the problem. I'm much happier in front of an easel or a lump of clay or a box full of beads and string. Art is my number one passion. Painting, sculpting, drawing, jewelry making — I love them all.

My other main passion is eating. Not just any food, though. It has to be absolutely horrible for your health. If sugar were flammable, my bedroom would be a major fire hazard. My parents forbid unhealthy eating, so I hide candy bars in my socks, bags of pretzels in my shoe boxes, cookies among my art supplies. (I also hide Nancy Drew books, because Mom and Dad think I should read only textbooks and Serious Literature.)

Believe it or not, I did once have a real soulmate in the Kishi family — my grandmother, Mimi. She really understood me. I've missed her terribly since she died, and I keep her picture on my bedroom wall for inspiration.

Mimi would have cracked up at my Ricky imitation.

Oh, well.

Snack time. I was definitely in a Yodels mood. I tromped upstairs and into my room.

Flinging my backpack onto the bed, I reached into my night table drawer and took out a fresh, unopened box of Yodels.

My clock read 5:10. In twenty minutes, my friends from the Baby-sitters Club would be coming over for a meeting (more about them later). I had just enough time to relax, eat, and do some homework. (Well, *think* about doing some homework, anyway.)

"Can't they take a suite in a hotel?" my mother's voice filtered in from down the hall.

"I couldn't very well ask them that, Rioko," my dad said. "Maybe they can't afford the rates. The point is, they're our friends, and they need a place to stay. Why are you so resistant?"

"I just don't think it's prudent, John."

I started giggling. I don't know why. I guess because "prudent" reminded me of "prunes." Anyway, I nearly choked on my Yodel.

"Prudent?" my dad repeated. "You're worried about what the people in town will think of us?"

"No, I meant on their part, John. I wonder if it's wise of them to come back to Stoneybrook. People still remember what happened at the lighthouse."

"Oh, come now. You and I know Alex didn't do anything wrong."

I stopped coughing.

What were they talking about?

The lighthouse? The old, graffiti-covered Stoneybrook lighthouse?

How weird. If Stoneybrook had a Most Ignored Building award, it would definitely go to that lighthouse. I guess boats used it in ancient times, but it had been boarded up for as long as I could remember. Kids say it's haunted, which I don't believe, of course. But the place definitely looks creepy, standing at the edge of an old jetty in the Sound, surrounded by a razor-wire fence.

Knowing my dad, whatever "happened" at the lighthouse probably had something to do with real estate or the stock market.

"Alex took the whole thing badly," Dad was saying. "His life has never been the same. Ever since the incident, his business ventures have all soured."

Hmmm. Alex must have been some crooked businessman. Some stock embezzler.

But why would my dad, the most conservative, law-abiding man in history, be friends with someone like that?

And why would he invite him to stay with us?

"If we say yes, where will we put them?" Mom was asking. "The kids aren't babies anymore. Little Stevie must be a teenager by now.

Not to mention Caryn and Laura . . . ."

Hold everything.

What a blast from the past. I knew who they were talking about. Caryn and Laura Hatt were these two little girls who used to live in Stoneybrook. They moved away when I was four or so, so I couldn't remember them too well. They had an older brother named Stevie. His two front teeth were missing and he used to call himself "Thtevie."

I also remember their dad, Mr. Hatt. He was cool. He used to tell us his first name was Cat-in-the. Was *he* Alex? (Rats, I had really believed him.)

"It'll just be for a little while," Dad said. "We should make them feel welcome in the community. When I think of the way they were driven out of town — "

"They weren't driven out," Mom replied. "They moved of their own free will."

I was standing against my half-open door, my ear pressed to the crack. Dying to hear more.

Just then the door swung open, smacking me against the wall.

"Yeow!" I cried out.

Janine barged into my room. "Have you seen my headband?"

"Have you heard of knocking?"

"The door was open."

"Janine, do you remember the Hatt family?" I blurted out.

Janine was now snooping around the room. "Sure. Mr. Hatt was Dad's friend."

"Really? Did he have anything to do with that old lighthouse?"

"He owned it," Janine replied.

"Yuck," I said. "Who'd want to own that disgusting place?"

"He owned a big chunk of waterfront property, I think. Dad helped him with some investments. Now, I know I wore it in here yesterday . . ."

"Listen, Janine, I heard Mom and Dad — "

"Did I take it off when I was using your phone?" Janine began rummaging through some art supplies, which lay in a heap on the floor.

"Janine, leave those alone! Your headband isn't here!"

"Well, if you'd keep your room neater — "

"If you wouldn't be so absentminded! Besides, what's the difference? You don't need a headband to listen to astroturfics."

"*Physics*. And I'm finished with that. I believe I've calculated the arrival time of the Veehoff Comet, which, in case you haven't heard, will be in eleven days."

"Congrats." *Haven't heard?* Everyone in

8

Stoneybrook was talking about the comet. I was already tired of it.

"We still haven't figured out if it'll hit," Janine continued. "Anyway, Jerry's coming over later and we're going to the movies."

That's another thing. Do you know what's worse than having a genius sister who makes you feel dumb and whom your parents love more than you?

Having a genius sister who makes you feel dumb and whom your parents love more than you, *who has a boyfriend!*

Grrrrr.

Not to be conceited or anything, but I'm talented, interesting, funny, and pretty. But do I have a boyfriend? Nooooo.

"Janine, I wish I could help you, but I was in the middle of cleaning up my room for the BSC meeting, and — "

"Can you lend me one?" Janine interrupted. "A headband, I mean. Nothing too, you know . . ."

"Funky?" I picked up a wide red headband with pairs of dice printed on it. "This one's pretty conservative."

Janine gave me a Look. "No solids?"

My clock read 5:25. Yikes. My friends were going to be arriving in five minutes. "What time is he coming?"

"Ten after eight, and Jerry's always on time."

"Ten after eight? You have three hours!"

"Two hours and forty-five minutes. But I have to do a calculus proof and begin building my three-dimensional enantiomer models for organic chemistry — "

"But it's Friday, Janine!"

"The best time to get a head start." Janine was pacing back and forth now, biting her fingernails. "Boys make everything so complicated."

"Uh-huh, I know what you mean." My clock clicked to 5:26. I began straightening up all the supplies Janine had knocked over.

"No, you don't. Sometimes I wish I'd never gotten involved with him."

So break up, I didn't say. "Yup. Uh, Janine? The BSC meeting's about to start. So would you — "

"Maybe a hat would work," Janine mused.

"Janiiiine! Go!"

"Okay, okay."

As she walked out, I could hear my parents, still arguing about the Hatts.

But I couldn't pay attention anymore. I was picking up wrappers and bottle caps and empty paint tubes.

My room was a sty. I had four minutes to make it gorgeous. Four minutes before the Friday meeting of the Baby-sitters Club.

CHAPTER 2

"Is it true," asked Stacey McGill, "that if the Veehoff Comet comes too close to Earth, people start turning into werewolves?"

"I heard it was vampires," Mallory Pike said.

"That's how it got its name." Abby Stevenson rose from the carpet, baring her teeth and talking in a Dracula accent. "Veehoff comet, vee hoff fool moon, and zo tonight vee hoff to sock your blod! Nyahh hahaha!"

Jessi Ramsey pretended to cower in fright. "Eeek!"

"That reminds me." I hopped off my bed and reached under it to pull out a box of chocolates. "Cherry creams!"

"Gross, Claudia," said Kristy Thomas. She pulled off the lid and grabbed three chocolates.

Abby took two. "The selection around here is going downhill."

"Yecchhh," Jessi said. "Could you pass them this way?"

Mallory reached for them, too. "Do you have caramels?"

"I'll check," I muttered.

Some gratitude.

As I rummaged through my closet, Mary Anne Spier said, "Last night, when I sat for Marilyn and Carolyn Arnold, they kept running over to the window to look for the comet."

"It's not supposed to come until the week after next," Kristy said.

Mary Anne laughed. "I tried to tell them, but they kept saying, 'How do you know?' "

"Comet feeeeever," Jessi sang. "Becca talks about it all the time, too."

"So do my brothers and sisters," Mallory said.

Stacey shrugged. "Hey, I don't blame them. How often does a comet like this come around?"

"Every seventy-one and a half years," Mary Anne replied. "We'll be in rockers for the next sighting."

"Janine's astrofistics class is trying to predict whether it'll hit the earth and wipe us all out," I said, pulling a candy box from among my hats. "Caramels?"

Mallory looked dismayed. "Don't scare me, Claudia."

"I thought you *wanted* caramels," I said.

"I meant the comet," Mallory replied.

"Astrofistics?" Abby murmured.

"Are we really in danger?" Jessi asked.

"Nahhhh," I said. "I just used some Comet in the bathroom. That stuff'll probably burn up in the atmosphere."

"Claudi*aaaa*," Stacey groaned.

"I have it!" Kristy piped up. "I have a great idea! On the night the Veehoff Comet appears, we can have a comet party for all our charges."

"Yyyyyes!" Abby exclaimed.

"Will we need a telescope?" Mary Anne asked.

"Janine has one," I volunteered.

"Don't even think about it!" Janine called from her room.

"First things first," Kristy said. "All in favor?"

"Ayyyyyye!"

It *was* a good idea. Which wasn't surprising, coming from Kristy. She's full of them.

Actually, if it weren't for one of her ideas, the Baby-sitters Club wouldn't exist.

It's kind of a cool story. I'll start at the beginning.

First, there was a Big Bang. Soon the earth and comets were formed. Then, one day, Kristy's mom was having trouble finding a sitter. So Kristy invented the Baby-sitters Club.

Okay, I left out a few details, but that's close enough. Kristy figured Stoneybrook would benefit from having a group of baby-sitters who met regularly at one central place. Then parents could reach several eager, reliable sitters with one convenient phone call.

The BSC started with only Kristy, Mary Anne, Stacey, and me, but we quickly grew to seven (ten, if you include our two associates and one honorary member).

Kristy set up the club like a business. Talk about organized. We pay dues, we write about each and every job in a notebook (which we all read regularly), and we have officers with special duties.

Our meetings are on Mondays, Wednesdays, and Fridays, from five-thirty to six. During those times, our clients call to request sitters.

What happens if they call during other times? They reach me, usually when I'm having a cow over my homework.

You see, my bedroom is the one-and-only official BSC headquarters, mainly because I'm the only member with her own private phone line.

Which makes me the club's host, head custodian, junk food caterer, and off-hours switchboard operator. All these duties are combined under one title: vice-president.

Kristy, naturally, is president. She runs the meetings, plans our events, dreams up advertising schemes, and makes us all feel horrible and guilty if we're late for anything.

As you can imagine, she's loud, smart, and full of energy. She's also short (barely five feet), athletic, and very casual. Super casual. Kristy is to fashion the way I am to astrophysics. Won't go near it. We practically have to force her into a dress for school dances.

Kristy's mind is very kid-centered. She always knows exactly what kids want. Take the comet party. No one but Kristy could have thought of that. Not long ago, when she realized that many of our younger charges wanted to play softball, Kristy organized a team for them. It's called Kristy's Krushers, and they play all the time during nice weather. Kristy even designed perfect antiboredom devices for us to take to jobs on rainy days. They're called Kid-Kits — boxes filled with old toys, games, and odds and ends. They don't sound like much, but kids adore them.

Kristy used to live across the street from me, with her parents and three brothers (Charlie's now seventeen, Sam's fifteen, and David Michael's seven). But just after David Michael was born, Kristy's life really changed. Her dad abandoned the family — walked out and never came back. Mrs. Thomas had to scramble to make a living and support four kids.

Things aren't quite so chaotic anymore. Mrs. Thomas remarried, to a divorced guy named Watson Brewer, who just happens to be a gazillionaire. Just like that — zoom! — Kristy was living in a mansion in Stoneybrook's chi-chi neighborhood.

Don't worry. Wealth hasn't changed Kristy. It's just given her more people to boss around. Watson's two children from his first marriage, seven-year-old Karen and four-year-old Andrew, live in the mansion during alternate months. Watson and Kristy's mom have a child of their own now, too — they adopted Emily Michelle, a two-year-old who was born in Vietnam. Kristy's grandmother, Nannie, moved in to help take care of her. The Brewer/Thomases also have lots of pets, so it's a pretty full house.

"The problem is," Kristy was saying, "where's the best place to see the comet?"

Rrrring!

A phone call cut off our astrowhatever discussion. Abby snatched up the receiver. "Hello, Baby-sitters Club? Veehoff vhat you need . . . No, Mrs. Hobart, it's just me, Abby. No, I'm not having allergies, just temporary in-

16

sanity. Sorry . . . okay, thanks, I'll call you back." She hung up the phone and announced: "The Hobarts, this Tuesday!"

"Who winds you up in the morning?" Kristy grumbled.

Mary Anne ran her finger along the BSC calendar. "You're available, Abby."

"I vood be honored," Abby replied. "I vill call her back!"

Vell, that's how the BSC operates. We run all job requests past Mary Anne, our secretary and keeper of the official BSC record book. She's responsible for knowing exactly who is free to sit. Sounds simple, right? No way. She has to mark a calendar with all our conflicts: dentist appointments, after-school activities, family commitments, rehearsals, practices, lessons, the works. Then, when requests come in, she tries to assign jobs evenly among us. In the back of the record book she maintains a client list with addresses, phone numbers, hourly rates, and house rules, along with their kids' special likes and dislikes, allergies, bedtimes, and so on.

I could never do her job. Just thinking about it gives me heart palpitations. To Mary Anne, though, it's no sweat. At a beach she could organize grains of sand by size.

She gets that ability from her dad. (We call him Richard, which is kind of a joke, since he's so formal.) According to Mary Anne, he lines up his socks, new to old, so they'll wear out evenly. When we were kids, I thought he was kind of mean. Boy, was he strict with Mary Anne. If you ask me, the problem was that he didn't have a wife to tell him to chill. (Mary Anne's mom died when Mary Anne was a baby.)

Anyway, Richard's a lot looser these days. Especially now that he's married again — to his old high school sweetheart, Sharon Porter Schafer, who happens to be the mom of another BSC member. Okay, okay, I'll backtrack. First, a girl named Dawn Schafer moved to Stoneybrook from California after her parents divorced. Dawn ended up joining the BSC and becoming good friends with Mary Anne. Together they discovered the secret history of Dawn's mom and Richard. So they played matchmaker and — *tssss!* — the old feelings were still hot. Wedding bells rang, and Mary Anne and her dad moved into the Schafers' rambling old farmhouse.

Happy ending? Not entirely. Dawn's younger brother hated Stoneybrook and moved back to California, and then Dawn became homesick and moved back, too (which is why she's now our honorary member).

Mary Anne was pretty broken up about Dawn's move. Mary Anne can be very sensitive, and shy, and sweet, and caring. She cries a lot. You might not expect someone so quiet to have a steady boyfriend, but she does. (His name is Logan Bruno.) You also wouldn't expect her to be best friends with Kristy the Mouth, but she is. Actually, Mary Anne and Kristy kind of look alike. Both are petite with brown hair and dark eyes. But Mary Anne cares a little more about fashion. She has a short, trendy hairstyle and wears preppier clothes than Kristy.

Our club treasurer is my best friend, Stacey. She collects dues and keeps the money in a manila envelope. Then, at the end of the month, she pays our expenses: my phone bill, Charlie Thomas's gas money (he drives Kristy and Abby to our meetings), supplies for Kid-Kits, and expenses for special events such as the comet party. If any money is left over, we sometimes have a pizza party for ourselves.

You would easily pick out Stacey in a BSC meeting. She's the only blonde, she wears the most stunning clothes, and she's the one member *not* stuffing candy into her face.

Sweets and Stacey are a very bad mix. She has a condition called diabetes. Don't ask me the biology of it, but it means her body goes ballistic over refined sugar. Too much sugar and she could become seriously ill, even pass out. Stacey can lead a normal life, as long as she eats at strictly regular times, stays away from sugar, and gives herself daily injections of something called insulin. I know, that last part sounds gross. Stacey says it isn't at all, though. (I think the no-sugar part is much worse.)

Stacey's incredible fashion sense comes from the streets of New York City. Well, not from the streets themselves. Mostly from boutiques and department stores. She actually grew up in the Big Apple, just a short subway ride from some of the greatest art galleries in the world. Do I sound jealous? I am. I happen to think NYC is the number one coolest place around (with the possible exception of the Ben & Jerry's ice cream factory in Vermont). Stacey visits New York often, because her dad still lives there (her parents are divorced).

Have you ever noticed that New York City is called "New York," but everywhere else in New York State is also called "New York"? I find this very distressing. For example, what does "native New Yorker" mean? Another of our members, Abby, was born and raised in a Long Island suburb, not far from New York City. So does that make her a "native New Yorker"? Or does that phrase refer to New York as in *New York City* New Yorkers, as opposed to New York as in *New York State* New

Yorkers? If you know the answer, please tell me.

Anyway, Abby is our newest member. Everything about her is wild. Her hair, for one thing. It's curly and dark and thick and always all over the place. Her sense of humor, for another. Her Ricky Ricardo imitation puts mine to shame. Her imitation of *me* puts me to shame. Honestly, she has so much talent and energy she could be a stand-up comic.

Well, maybe not. The stage would have to be dust free. Abby is allergic to dust — and pollen, and shellfish, and strawberries, and fur, and about a million other things. She also has asthma, for which she carries around inhalers. Despite all this, she is the BSC's most talented athlete. (Don't ever tell Kristy I said that; Kristy's a little jealous of her.)

Abby, her twin sister, and their mom moved into a house near Kristy's, soon after Dawn moved to California. It was great timing. We badly needed another sitter by then. We were hoping Abby's sister, Anna, would join us, too, but she turned us down. She's a serious music student who practices her violin every day for hours.

The Stevensons are Jewish. Recently all us BSC members attended Abby's and Anna's Bat Mitzvah. That's a coming-of-age ritual thirteen-year-old Jewish girls go through, and the ceremony was very moving. They had to recite in Hebrew, and they didn't even make one mistake. (At least they said they didn't.) The only sad part part was that their dad couldn't see them. He died in a car accident when they were nine. Abby never talks about him. I guess the memory is still too painful.

Abby, by the way, is our alternate officer. That means she substitutes whenever another officer is absent. She became president for awhile, when Kristy was on vacation in Hawaii with her family. Right away Abby abolished dues and loosened up the rules. That didn't last long, but when Kristy found out, she nearly had a heart attack. (Ask me if I think Kristy will ever go on vacation again.)

All of the BSC members I've mentioned so far are thirteen. All are in eighth grade at Stoneybrook Middle School . . . except me, of course. Boy, do I miss having them in my classes. But I try to look on the bright side. If I'm left back again, then next year I'll be in the same grade as our two junior officers, Jessica Ramsey and Mallory Pike.

Jessi and Mallory are eleven. Their parents will not let them baby-sit at night, unless it's for their own siblings. Jessi and Mal grumble about this all the time. They call it Oldest Child Syndrome, meaning that parents are strictest with oldest children and more lenient with younger ones. (Ha. They should live in my house for awhile.) Maybe the "syndrome" explains why they're both great sitters: they have lots of practice at home. Jessi has two younger siblings, and Mal has seven (yup, seven, including triplets).

Anyway, the grumbling is one of the many things that keeps them close friends. Another is reading horse books (they're both absolute fanatics). And each of them is incredibly creative. Mallory likes to write and illustrate her own stories, and Jessi's a phenomenal ballet dancer.

Mallory has white skin and thick, reddish-brown hair. She wears glasses and braces (both of which she absolutely hates). Jessi has chocolate-brown skin, is thin and graceful, and usually wears her hair pulled back tightly in a bun.

Jessi's family moved to Stoneybrook from a racially mixed neighborhood in Oakley, New Jersey. As African-Americans, they discovered how prejudiced some people can be in a mostly white place like Stoneybrook. (Boy, could I relate to that. I mean, most Stoney-brookites are cool, but it only takes a few to make life miserable.)

Now you know all our regular members. We have three irregular members, too. Our two associates, Logan Bruno (MaryAnne's boyfriend, remember?) and Shannon Kilbourne, fill in for us when we're overloaded with jobs. They're not required to attend meetings or pay dues. Logan has blondish-brown hair, speaks with a slight Kentucky accent, and is involved in tons of after-school sports. Shannon goes to a private school called Stoneybrook Day School, where she belongs to every extracurricular group ever invented.

Dawn Schafer, our honorary member, belongs to another baby-sitting group in Palo City, California. It's called the We ♥ Kids Club, and because it's Kristy-less, it's much more casual than the BSC. I miss Dawn a lot. She's really independent and outspoken, especially about her interest in health foods and ecology. These things are not exactly at the top of my priority list, but I admire Dawn for sticking to her guns and not caring what anyone thinks.

Okay, back to the meeting. Our leader, Kristy, was at sixes and sevens about the comet party. (Did you ever wonder why "at sixes and sevens" means *confused*? Why not "twelves and thirteens," or "math in general"?)

"Brenner Field would be a good viewing spot for the comet," Kristy said, "except it might not be dark enough, with all the streetlights surrounding it."

Mary Anne nodded. "The darker it is, the better you can see the comet."

"The Sound is really dark at night," Mallory suggested.

"The lighthouse!" I blurted out.

"Right," Kristy said. "We'll cut the razor wire, pry off the lock, then saw through the planks on the window."

"Boy, is that place ugly," Stacey remarked. "It sticks out like a sore thumb."

Mallory grimaced. "More like a severed thumb."

"Severed thumbs don't stick out," Abby said. "I think they just lie flat."

"Gross," Mary Anne said.

"I hear it's haunted," Jessi volunteered. "The ghost of some murdered kid, I think."

"Well, the people who own that lighthouse are coming to stay with us," I went on. "The Hatt family."

"I know them," Abby said, nodding solemnly. "Porkpie, Slouch, Stovepipe, and Top."

"Ha ha," Kristy snapped. "I remember them, Claud. They used to visit your house when we were little. Whatever happened to them, anyway?"

I shrugged. "They moved away. I overheard my mom and dad talking about them, and it sounds like Mr. Hatt got into some trouble. Something about the lighthouse. All I know is,

Mom really didn't want the Hatts to stay with us."

"They were probably chased out by the Stoneybrook Beautification Society," Stacey commented, "for owning a hideous eyesore."

"My dad says it was nice once," Mary Anne said. "It was only closed down after the bad stuff happened."

"What bad stuff?" I asked.

"I don't know, exactly," Mary Anne replied. "But I remember driving by there with my dad one night when I was little. We hit lots of traffic, and we started singing 'Fox Went Out on a Chilly Night.' As we went past the lighthouse, I saw flashing lights everywhere — all these police cars and ambulances. Dad stuck his head out the window and talked to a policeman for awhile. I couldn't understand what they were saying, but boy, did Dad's mood change. After they finished talking, his face was so stiff and gray and serious. He totally forgot about our song."

"Did you ask him what had happened?" I said.

Mary Anne nodded. "I sure did. And he refused to tell me. But I kept asking, 'Was it something bad?' over and over. Finally he answered, 'Yes, Mary Anne, very bad. Not something for a little girl to know about.' Well, of course, that made me even more curious. But

I was kind of frightened, too. You know me. At that age, I couldn't even watch Disney cartoons. So I asked, 'Was it something scary, too?' And I'll never forget his reaction . . ." Mary Anne's voice trailed off. She bit her lip, frowning.

We were all leaning toward her, like paper clips around a magnet. "Well?" I asked.

"All he said was, 'Mary Anne, you must never, *ever* go someplace where you know you're not supposed to be, no matter how old you are.' "

"What did that mean?" I asked.

Mary Anne shook her head. "I was so scared, I didn't ask. Neither of us ever talked about it again."

My throat felt like beach sand on a hot day. I gulped and nearly choked.

Parts of my parents' argument floated in my brain: *We know Alex did nothing wrong . . . I wonder if it's wise for them to come back to Stoneybrook . . . they were driven out of town . . .*

I looked at my doorknob. I wondered how much a big, heavy-duty lock would cost.

CHAPTER 3

"Pass the brown stuff," I said.

My mom handed me a steaming platter. "Beef teriyaki," she reminded me, with a raised eyebrow.

Dad spooned himself some green beans from another platter, then held it out to Janine. "Your favorite, beans sautéed with garlic."

"Not tonight," Janine said. "I'm going out with Jerry. The last thing I need is halitosis."

"I'm sure Mom *washed* them beforehand," I said.

Janine gave me a Look. "Excuse me?"

"Besides, I think that only happens with, like, undercooked pork," I went on.

"That's *trichinosis*," Janine said. "Halitosis is bad breath."

I handed her the beef. "Here. This smells great."

Janine shook her head. "Too heavy. It'll

make my stomach flutter. I'll stick with plain rice."

"Since when did you become so boy crazy?" I asked.

"Someday you'll know how this feels," Janine replied.

Oh, puh-leeze.

I ladled globs of food onto my plate. "Mmmm, Mom and Dad. This dinner is sooooo delicious. Yum yum."

I know, I was being cruel. But think of it. Janine was lucky enough to be going out on a Friday night date. The least she could do was not fuss about it in front of me.

"Well, girls," my dad said, wiping his mouth with his napkin, "I have some news. Today I spoke on the phone with Alex Hatt. Does that name ring a bell?"

Gulp.

It sure did. An alarm bell.

"Claudia was talking about him earlier," Janine piped up. "She said — "

"I said I wondered what ever happened to him!" I interrupted her. Leave it to Janine to tell my parents I'd been eavesdropping. I glared at her, but she was looking at her watch.

"Um, may I be excused?" Janine asked.

"Jerry's not going to be here for twenty minutes," Mom said. "Calm down, sweetheart. Your father has something important to say."

Dad cleared his throat. "Yes. Well, as you both know, the Hatts are old, dear friends. Since their move to Arizona, I've stayed in touch with Alex. The bad news is that his business hasn't gone well, and his wife has been laid off from her job. The good news is that the family would like to move back to Stoney-brook. They have real estate here and have always loved the area. They've even arranged places for their children in the schools. However, staying in a hotel while they look for a place to live would be a big financial strain. So, taking into account the fact that their kids are about your age, I thought we'd help them out. Your mother and I have invited them to stay with us for a couple of weeks. They'll be arriving on Sunday — "

"Sunday?" I repeated. "That's in two days!"

"Your math is improving," Janine murmured.

"What happens if they can't find a house?" I asked.

Mom shrugged. "We'll host them for a month, if that's what it takes. We've agreed that if things become uncomfortable, they'll move to a hotel. They are friends in need, after all . . ."

"But that's . . . five people!"

"Excellent, Claudia," Janine interjected.

"Will you stop it?" I snapped. "Where will we put them?"

"Well, Mr. and Mrs. Hatt will sleep in the den," Mom replied. "Your aunt Peaches and uncle Russ were quite comfortable there when they were visiting."

"Their boy, Steve, will stay in Mimi's old room," Dad added.

I felt a tug in my chest, picturing a toothless, smudge-faced kid in my grandmother's bedroom.

"I'd like to put Laura and Caryn in Janine's room," Mom went on.

"Wait a minute," Janine said. "Where will I sleep?"

I grinned. Poor Janine, without a room. "The kitchen table's comfortable," I said, "or maybe there's a spare attic room at Jerry's."

"I thought you two would stay together in Claudia's room," Mom said cheerily.

I felt as if I'd been hit over the head with a baseball bat. *"Whaaaaaat?"*

Dad smiled. "You have to promise, no late-night chitchat!" he said with a chuckle.

"You can't — " I sputtered.

"I can't — " Janine added.

"I know, it'll be tight," Mom said. "Claudia, you'll have to clear out a corner for Janine's computer — "

"No way!" The words finally exploded out of me. "I can't live in the same room with her!"

"Claudia, she's your sister," Mom said.

And she will drive me absolutely out of my mind, I wanted to scream.

"But the room is crowded already," I pleaded, "and I need space to do my art, and besides, what about the Baby-sitters Club?"

"Exactly!" Janine agreed. "I can't be expected to concentrate with a room full of nattering girls — "

"We do not *natter!*" I shot back. "Whatever that means."

Janine folded her arms tightly. "It just won't work!"

"Why not put one of the sisters in my room," I suggested, "and the other in Janine's?"

Mom shook her head. "Apparently Laura and Caryn refuse to be separated."

"Look, I know it will be a difficult adjustment at first," Dad said. "But keep in mind it's quite temporary."

"It might even be fun," Mom added.

"Fun?" Janine and I both groaned at the same time.

I could tell Dad was reaching his patience limit. His smile had faded into a small, tight line. "When I was starting out in business, struggling to make ends meet, Alex Hatt was one of the only people who helped me. I have never forgotten it. Now his family needs our support, and they'll have it. Would you pass the rice, please?"

So that was it. No arguments, no nothing. The Hatts were coming, and I was going to share a room with my geeky sister. I could just picture it: Janine lecturing me about my study habits. Stepping on my paint tubes. Complaining about my radio. Clacking away on her computer keyboard while I'm trying to concentrate. Finding my hidden candy bars. Tattling on me. Refusing to leave during BSC meetings. Making everybody feel stupid.

No. No. *No!* I would run away from home before agreeing to this. That would convince them.

I thought of the money I'd saved up. That would take me as far as New York. Maybe I could call Stacey's dad, and he could find me a cheap apartment. I'd pretend to be eighteen and sell my paintings in Central Park.

I braced myself. In my mind I worded my announcement. I stood up and prepared to let them all have it.

Mom and Dad looked at me curiously. Janine was downing a glass of milk.

The teriyaki aroma wafted up to me. My mouth began to water.

I ladled some more on my plate and sat

down again. Tomorrow I'd run away.

Janine angrily slapped her milk glass down on the table. Unfortunately it was a little too close to the edge. It spilled over onto her skirt.

Her nice Friday-night-date skirt.

"Aaaaugh! I have to change!"

Janine bolted up from the table. As she raced upstairs, Mom and Dad gave her sympathetic glances. Me, I munched quietly on my beef.

Served her right, I thought. (I'm not sure why. It just did.)

The rest of dinner was a snoozefest. Mom hardly said a word. She seemed a little shell-shocked by the way Janine and I had reacted. Dad had that *don't-think-of-trying-to-change-my-mind* look, so I didn't bring up the Hatts again.

By the time Janine came back downstairs, we were starting to clear the table.

"We left your plate," Mom called out. "I'll put it in the microwave — "

"No, thanks," Janine replied from the living room. "I'm not hungry anymore."

I cleared her plate, loaded the dishwasher, and wiped off the table. What did Janine do to help? Nada. Zip. When I went into the living room, she was staring out the front window. "I guess looking for Jerry is more important than cleaning up," I grunted.

"How do I look?" she asked.

She was wearing a gray pleated wool skirt

and a white Oxford button-down longsleeve shirt. "Very clean," I replied.

"He should be here by now. The movie starts in fifteen minutes."

Guess what? Jerry didn't show up at his promised time, 8:10. Or at 8:20. Or 8:30.

By 8:45, Janine was a train wreck. Her face was all red, and she was pacing the living room like a caged but very smart beast. "How can he do this to me?" she muttered. "Does he think I have time to waste?"

"Call him," I suggested. "Maybe something happened."

"I hope it was awful." Janine looked at her watch. "I'll give him another couple of minutes."

I was in my room, working on a still-life sketch of a bowl of chips, when the family phone rang.

"Janine, it's Jerry!" I heard my mom call from downstairs.

My clock read 8:58. I ran to the top of the stairs and listened. (I know. What a sneak.)

"Where have you been?" was Janine's greeting. "What do you mean, *forgot?* . . . You'd better be sorry! Do you realize how much I could have accomplished in this time? . . . I'm too tired right now, and it's late. . . . No, I'm going to get ready for bed. Good night!"

SMACK went the receiver into the hook.

Thump! Thump! Thump! went her footsteps as she headed for the stairs.

I scurried back into my room, sat at my art table, and pretended to be drawing.

"He says he forgot!" Janine snarled as she passed my open door. "*Forgot!* Can you believe it? Oooooh, I hate boys!"

She ran into her room and slammed the door. Moments later, classical music was blaring from her speakers.

"Hrrrm hm haaaa . . ." she hummed along tunelessly.

Tack-tack-tackety-tack! banged her fingers on the computer keyboard.

I slumped into my chair.

My parents expected me to room with *that?*

Over my dead body.

CHAPTER 4

Sunday was moving day.

My body was not dead. In fact, I had to help Janine move into my room.

Which felt sort of like drilling the cavities in my own teeth.

I knew that rearranging the room for Janine's stuff would be a family affair. I'd spent the morning in search of my hidden junk food, and then crammed it all into the back of my closet. The last thing in the world I needed was for my parents to discover my secret.

Dad backed into the room, helping Janine carry in her computer desk. He glanced over his shoulder and announced, "Looks like you'll need to move the bed over a bit."

Mom and I ran around to the other side of my bed, hooked our fingers under the frame, and pulled.

Janine and Dad shimmied the computer desk into the corner.

"It's too cramped," Janine grumbled.

"I agree," I agreed.

"You'll survive," was Mom's reply.

A spare bed was already against the other wall — where my easel had been. The easel was now wedged in another corner with my art desk, just beyond my sweets-packed closet.

My heart was breaking. My room looked like a storage closet. My escape, my studio, my own little world — shattered. On my wall shelves, beautiful art books were side-by-side with titles such as *Fundamentals of Thermodynamics* and *Programming Tips for DOS Users*.

Only a few weeks . . .

Only a few weeks . . .

I kept repeating those words to myself.

"What's that smell?" Mom asked.

"What smell?"

Mom sniffed, looking toward the closet. "It's sweet. Chocolatey. Don't you smell it?"

Yikes!

"Smells normal to me," I replied, which was sort of the truth.

I have heard the brain has amazing powers. I once saw a TV show about a girl who could make objects move just by concentrating on them.

I willed my closet door to close.

Over my dead body, it seemed to answer.

Whock! Whock!

From outside my window I heard the smack of car doors. We all ran to look.

A minivan was parked at the curb. I recognized Mr. and Mrs. Hatt, who were each holding wrapped presents. The kids, however, looked totally unfamiliar. Especially the tall, wavy-haired teenaged guy with the high cheekbones and the ripped jeans jacket.

"Is that *Thtevie?*" Janine asked.

"Janine, don't you dare say that to his face," I warned her.

Mom and Dad were already running downstairs, leaving the chocolate smell behind. I slammed my closet door and ran after them with Janine.

Dad was the first one out the front door. "Alex! Flora! What a pleasure!" he exclaimed.

Mr. and Mrs. Hatt were beaming. They threw their arms around my parents, saying how little they'd all changed. (Which was a lie. Mr. Hatt, for one thing, had been neither fat nor bald, as I recall.)

Mrs. Hatt gasped when she saw me. "Goodness, this must be Janine!"

"No!" I yelped. "I'm Claudia."

"Little Dodee-a!" Mrs. Hatt exclaimed. "You're so grown-up!"

Dodee-a? That was worse than Thtevie.

All the adults gushed and mushed over everybody. We kids stood there in Duh-ville, smiling and nodding politely.

Ecthept Thtevie. He kept looking angrily up and down the street, as if he were expecting someone he didn't particularly like.

He did talk a little, though, to my mom. She said, "What a handsome young man! I'll bet no one calls you Stevie anymore."

"Uh-uh," he said. "Steve."

The corners of his lips turned up a fraction of an inch. That tiny motion brought his whole face to life. His eyes were gray-blue, like a winter morning sky. They cut right through the long lock of brown hair that hung over his forehead.

He looked at me for about about a millionth of a second, then looked back up the street.

A millionth of a second was enough.

Maybe these next few weeks wouldn't be so horrible after all.

"We'll show Mr. and Mrs. Hatt and Steve where they'll be staying," Mom was saying. "Claudia and Janine, why don't you take Caryn and Laura upstairs? But come right down, because it's lunchtime."

"Sure," I said, tearing my eyes away from you-know-who.

Caryn smiled shyly at me. She had curly blonde hair, freckled skin, and a friendly face.

I remembered her as a toddler. It was hard to believe this was she.

Janine was already leading Laura inside. Caryn and I followed.

"You two will be sharing my room," Janine explained as we walked upstairs. "I've locked my filing cabinets, but please make sure not to touch my telescope or flip the metal compartments on any of my diskettes. Feel free to read any paperbacks, though."

My sister. What a generous soul.

We walked into Janine's room. Her bed and a cot were freshly made up, side by side. That looked kind of cute. Unfortunately, though, Janine hadn't done anything to spruce up her room. It looked very . . . well, Janine-ish. Kind of drab and colorless.

Staring down from the walls were black-and-white posters of Janine's heroes. Laura was gazing at them. "Who are they?" she asked.

Janine began pointing. "Madame Curie, Virginia Woolf, Einstein, Mozart, Richard Feynman, Doris Lessing, Galileo . . ."

Laura looked as if she'd suddenly found herself on Mars.

"It's really nice of you to give us your room," Caryn said softly.

Janine smiled. "No problem at all."

"Mmm-hm," I lied.

Laura leaned over Janine's bed and pushed the mattress with one finger, as if she were poking an animal to see if it was dead or alive.

"What grade are you guys in?" Caryn asked.

"Eleventh, putatively," Janine said.

Laura snorted a laugh. "Puta-what?"

"Meaning I will graduate with the eleventh-grade class, although I take primarily college-level courses."

I was cringing inside. Why couldn't Janine learn how to talk like a normal kid?

"I'm in seventh," I added.

"Me, too," Laura said. "Funny, you look older than twelve."

"She was sent back," Janine said flatly.

"You *were?*" Laura exclaimed.

"Yes." I gave my sister a *let's-change-the-topic-right-now* look and spun toward Caryn. "And how old are *you?*"

"Ten," Caryn replied. "I'm in fifth grade."

"It must be disorienting to change schools in the middle of the year," Janine said.

"We couldn't help it," Caryn said. "We had to move, sort of."

I nodded. "I heard. Your mom lost her job, huh?"

"Yes, but that wasn't the reason," Caryn replied. "It was mostly because of what Steve did at school — "

"Caryn, that's not true!" Laura snapped.

"They said they were going to expel him," Caryn said. "I heard Mom talking to the principal."

"Steve got into a little trouble, that's all," Laura explained with a tight smile. "It wasn't his fault, and it's not the main reason we're thinking of moving back here."

"Lunch is served!" my dad called from downstairs.

Laura took her sister's arm and led her out of the room.

I looked at Janine. She shrugged.

"All I know," she whispered, "is that he's cute."

With a giggle, she left the room.

Cute?

I stood there in shock.

I wanted to scream.

I wanted to rip down Einstein, crumple him up into a ball, and throw him at Janine.

She'd taken half my room. She'd made me feel like a total dork in front of our guests. She'd dragged me down with all her complaints about her boyfriend.

And now, just when I might have met the boy of my dreams, what did she want to do? Take him away!

Easy, Kishi, I told myself. You are taking this way too seriously. It's not a big deal. Steve was a total stranger, anyway. And maybe he wasn't such a nice guy. Who knew what awful deed he'd done in his previous school?

Oh, well, one thing was certain. No way would a guy like that be interested in Janine.

I ran downstairs. Mom and Dad had already set out the cold cuts and bakery bread they'd bought that morning. Janine took out a big bowl of potato salad, which she and I had whipped up ourselves. I filled a bowl with Cape Cod potato chips, as an appetizer.

Before long we were all sitting at the dining room table, grazing away.

Well, except for Laura. "You don't have, like, tuna salad or something?" she asked.

"I'll make some," Mom said, leaping up.

"Please, don't fuss," Mrs. Hatt said. Then she smiled sharply at Laura. "Honey, have cold cuts. You like them."

Laura rolled her eyes. "I did when I was eleven."

"No fuss at all!" Mom called from the kitchen.

I had grown sick of sampling the potato salad while I was making it. But the bowl happened to be in front of Steve, who was sitting to my right. Suddenly those potatoes looked mighty tempting.

"Mind if I take some?" I asked.

Steve kind of grunted. As I reached over, I smiled at him.

He caught my glance for a moment, then looked back down at his roast beef sandwich.

"So . . ." Mr. Hatt said. "How are things in Stoneybrook?"

"Property values are going up." Dad let out a laugh. "If you fixed up your piece and sold it, I think you'd make a tidy profit!"

"If someone would ever buy it," Mrs. Hatt said wearily. "I think we should hire a demolition team. Who needs all the reminders — "

Mr. Hatt suddenly dropped his fork on the floor. "Oh, sorry, I'll get another."

"No, let me." Dad sprang up and went into the kitchen.

Mr. Hatt sat back in his seat. He shot his wife a strong Look.

An extremely strong Look.

"So, you still own the lighthouse property?" Janine asked.

"Yes," Mr. Hatt replied.

"You're kidding!" I blurted out.

Mrs. Hatt laughed. "Hard to believe someone would just let it sit there and rot, huh?"

"No," I said. "I mean, yeah. I mean, I guess I never thought anyone would, you know, *want* that place."

Duh. Stick the old Doc Martens right in your mouth, Claudia.

"Actually, we hope to sell the land," Mr. Hatt said. "Or fix it up and rent it. That's one of the reasons we want to move back."

"He's paying taxes on that land!" Dad shouted from the kitchen. "See, it's sort of like Monopoly."

"First we have to see if the building is in good enough shape," Mrs. Hatt said. "We drove by on the way here, and it doesn't seem too sturdy."

"Sure it does," Steve mumbled. "It's cool."

(Aha! Two full sentences! Hope!)

"I think it's disgusting," Laura said.

Steve grinned. "I'm going to have a party there . . . after dark."

"He's been saying that all week," Caryn whispered to me.

"Well, *I* wouldn't go to it," Laura said.

"I wouldn't invite you," Steve retorted.

"Kids," Mr. Hatt scolded. "Nobody goes in there until we search it thoroughly."

"It's been boarded up tight for years," Steve said. "What do you expect to find? Dead bodies?"

"Steven, stop that!" Mrs. Hatt snapped.

I wasn't sure, but I thought I saw her shiver.

I, Claudia, am no fool. Something weird was going on. I could smell it. I knew it had to do with the lighthouse — and the Hatts were involved.

Just who were we living with, anyway?

CHAPTER 5

"Don't tell me," Laura whispered. "You don't know who that is, either. Right?"

We were on our way out of last-period English. Laura gestured toward a blonde girl who was leaving the room in front of us. The girl was surrounded by three guys, all laughing at something she'd said.

"Well, I know she's on the cheerleading team," I whispered back. "Her name's Barbara or Bonnie or Bobbi or something. I'm sorry, Laura. Most of my friends are in eighth grade. I don't know too many seventh-graders yet."

"Yeah, like one percent."

I couldn't understand Laura. She was too shy to introduce herself to anybody. And yet the only people she wanted to meet were the super-popular kids. Plus, she was always so snippy with me — and I was trying very hard to be nice to her.

You wouldn't have believed her at lunchtime. She would not stop staring at the jock table, even though we were sitting at the opposite end of the cafeteria.

As we walked into the hallway, Laura pulled a compact out of her bag and looked at herself in the mirror.

"Gag me," she said. "I'm going to the bathroom. Come with me."

As soon as we entered the girls' room, Laura set some makeup out on the sink ledge. In her hurry, her sleeve brushed against an open tube of lipstick. It fell to the floor, jamming into a marble tile.

"Ohhhh, look at that!" she said angrily.

Have you ever seen a tube of lipstick splatted flat on a floor? It's pretty funny. I couldn't help laughing.

"Some help you are!" Laura said, rummaging around in her bag again. "I feel like an alien here. I thought I'd be meeting people. I thought that by now people would at least know who I am!"

"It's only your first day," I reminded her.

"Yeah, but I have to stick with you, right? And you don't know anybody. So how am I going to gashanomeboppy?"

She said that last part while she was putting on lipstick from another tube. I never did find out what she said. Frankly, I didn't care.

"There!" she finally announced, appraising herself in the mirror. "I'm human!"

I could have argued, but hey, a guest is a guest.

Out into the crowded hallway we went. We stopped at our lockers for our coats and headed outside.

During breakfast, Mr. Hatt had offered to pick us up from school. Sure enough, he and Caryn were waiting in the Hatt family mini-van at the curb.

Laura and I climbed into the backseat. "Thanks for picking us up," I said.

"Don't thank me yet," Mr. Hatt replied as he started up the car. "I'm going to drag you on some errands. Shouldn't take too long. I need to pick up some exterior paint for the light-house."

"You decided to renovate it?" I asked.

"Yup!" Caryn piped up. "Isn't that cool?"

"I spent most of the morning trying to get into the place," Mr. Hatt said. "Between the rusted locks and chains, the fallen razor wire, the wooden planks, and the shutters I thought I'd never see the inside."

"What was it like?" I asked.

Mr. Hatt smiled. "I'll let you see for your-self."

I gulped. "We're going there now?"

"O-o-oh, no! You're not taking me to that old rat hole!" Laura declared.

"Scared?" Caryn asked with a smile.

Laura stuck out her tongue.

"It's in pretty good shape," Mr. Hatt said. "I had a structural engineer look at it. Okay with you, Claudia?"

"Uh, sure, but I have to be back by five-thirty for a Baby-sitters Club meeting."

"No sweat."

He drove us to the hardware store. When I heard him ask the clerk for ten cans of flat white, I almost gagged.

"It'll look like the abominable snowman!" I blurted out. "Do you have an old picture of the lighthouse?"

Mr. Hatt shrugged. "Sure."

Claudia the Color Freak to the rescue. Mr. Hatt's photo was black-and-white, but I noticed the lighthouse had trim around the middle. It cried out for two tones — a red-and-white motif, maybe. I looked at paint samples for awhile and picked out a soft sand color for the top, a crimson for the bottom. Warm but vibrant. Soothing to the eyes but strongly attractive.

"How do you know so much about color?" Laura asked as we loaded the cans of paint into the car.

50

"Look into her room sometime," Caryn said. "She's a great artist."

At least I had one friend in the Hatt family.

As Mr. Hatt turned onto Shore Drive, I heard the screech of a seagull. The sun was hanging low over the Sound, swollen and dusky orange in the mist. Birds flew across it, their silhouettes black as bats.

Even with the windows closed and the car's heater turned up, I could smell the salty air. As we pulled around a bend in the road, the lighthouse came into view, just north of us. In the dim rays of the setting sun, the jagged graffiti looked like snakes crawling up the walls.

The lighthouse window faced south, looking out over the Sound. We could see it for a moment, before the road curved around the lighthouse to the north.

In that moment I thought I saw movement through the window.

"Is . . . anyone in there?" I asked.

"Not that I know of," Mr. Hatt replied.

The radio was tuned to an all-news station, blathering on and on about hideous crimes and bad economic news. I desperately wanted Mr. Hatt to change the station, but I kept my mouth shut.

Go home.

My brain shot me the message. I was suddenly cold, tired, and hungry. And the BSC meeting was only forty-five minutes away. What were we doing in this place?

We pulled to a stop in front of the main gate.

"Have fun," Laura said sullenly, her arms folded.

As Mr. Hatt, Caryn, and I climbed out, the wintry wind made me shiver. A distant buoy chimed dully over the water.

Big wooden boards lay around the base of the lighthouse. The one window, on the second floor, was now a dark, square hole.

"We have just enough light to see the inside, I think," Mr. Hatt said, strolling up the front walkway.

"There's . . . no light in there?" I asked.

Mr. Hatt chuckled. "Not until I call the electrical company."

My knees locked. What if rats lived in there? Or bats? Or worse?

EEEEEEEAAAAAAGGGHH!

I nearly jumped out of my skin at the noise.

I spun around. A seagull was swooping down. Caryn was tossing pieces of a candy bar onto the ground.

I swallowed. Bravely I turned and followed Mr. Hatt into the lighthouse.

Something brushed against my eyebrows as I walked through the front door. I wiped my fingers across my face and peeled off a layer of cobwebs.

Mr. Hatt was standing to my right. The first-floor space was huge, much larger than it looked from outside. In the middle of the floor, a wooden spiral staircase wound upward from a basement, right on through to the second floor and the roof. Although the lighthouse was round, the floor was an odd shape, because of a small room on the right.

"Can Claudia and I explore?" Caryn asked.

I looked up into the pitch-black hole of the stairwell. I gulped so loudly I sounded like a bullfrog.

Me? Up there with the ghost?

Uh-uh. Not in this life. (Or any other.)

"Hang on." Mr. Hatt disappeared into the room and emerged with two flashlights. "I stored these earlier."

He handed the flashlights to Caryn, then scurried downstairs to the basement.

"Caryn," I whispered. "I saw something move up there!"

"Cool!" she exclaimed.

"*Cool?*"

But she was already heading for the stairs. And I was about to be alone.

I ran after her. "Hey, give me one of those flashlights!"

The old wooden steps creaked as we climbed. The frozen, rusty metal banister seemed to stick to my hand, and I wished that I'd worn gloves.

"Creepy," Caryn said, stepping onto the second floor.

I climbed up beside her and shone the light around. Metal instruments like giant, petrified insects lay heaped against the wall. Above us, a lightbulb hung limply from a wire. Just beyond it, where the wall met the ceiling, our light beams made dancing patterns of the thick cobwebs.

Through the square window I could see the sun flattening into a half circle against the horizon. I knelt by the sill and watched.

Have you ever seen the sun set on the water? You can actually see it move. It's hypnotizing.

"I'm heeeeeere . . ."

I clutched my flashlight at the sound of the voice. It was muffled and low-pitched. It sounded male, but it was not Mr. Hatt's deep, gruff tone. It was the voice of a young man.

Was it Steve? Had he walked over to see us?

"Hello?" I called out.

Clank! A metallic noise answered, as if someone had bumped against one of the old contraptions.

54

I shone my flashlight around. The entire second floor was empty. "Caryn, was that you?" I said. "Caryn, this isn't funny!"

"I'm up here!" she called from the roof. "Come see this light!"

Funny. I hadn't even heard her walk up there.

I climbed the stairs through a trapdoor opening and onto the roof. The fresh air felt wonderful, and I could hear the water's rhythmic lapping against the dock. Around us was a wall about four feet high. In the center of the floor was a huge cylindrical pivot that supported an enormous double light, like giant car headlights, back-to-back.

"Did you just hear someone?" I asked.

"Yes," Caryn said. "You."

"But no one else? Not your brother?"

A distant voice filtered up from outside. *What in Sam Hill are you doing here?*

There was no mistaking that. Caryn and I clattered down the spiral stairs.

Mr. Hatt was standing just outside the lighthouse. A craggy-faced man in a red-checked wool coat was walking across the small, scrubby lawn toward him.

"Mr. Langley!" Mr. Hatt said. "Long time no see — "

"Not long enough!" the man retorted.

"Well, uh, I was just — just opening up the lighthouse," Mr. Hatt stuttered. "Trying to figure out what to do with it."

Even in the darkness I could see how red Mr. Langley's face was. "I thought you'd at least have the decency to wait until I was six feet under before you showed yourself around here, Hatt."

"Perhaps I should have called — " Mr. Hatt began.

"What do you think I'd have said?" Mr. Langley growled. " 'Come on over, all is forgiven'? 'Come peel the scabs off the wound'?"

Caryn and I were frozen in the doorway. Laura was now standing by the car, watching.

"I'm sorry, Mr. Langley," Mr. Hatt said. "I know how you must feel, but you have to understand that I do bear responsibility for the property and the — "

Mr. Langley scrunched up his face and spat.

Mr. Hatt jumped back as a plug of saliva hurtled through the air and landed at his feet.

"Go back to where you belong," Mr. Langley said, stalking away.

CHAPTER 6

I was really looking forward to sitting Tuesday for the Hobarts. I couldn't believe how mild it was today. Not exactly shrimp-on-the-bahhhbie weather, more a football-and-hot-chocolate afternoon.

Did I expect I'd be worrying about rats in the streets? NOOOOOO...

I should explain something first. When Abby wrote "bahhhbie," she meant *barbie*. No, not the doll. The grill.

You see, the Hobarts are from Australia. "Shrimp on the barbie" is Australian for "shrimp on the barbecue." Abby was trying to imitate the Hobarts' pronunciation.

(Always the mimic, even on paper.)

The Hobart boys love sports. That can make life a little tough for sitters like me, but they are probably Logan Bruno's favorite charges. Kristy's too. And since Abby joined the BSC, the Hobarts have been in baby-sitter heaven.

All four of them — Ben, who's eleven, James (eight), Mathew (six), and Johnny (four) — have bright, reddish-blond hair and freckled faces. If you morphed their faces, youngest to oldest, it would look like one boy growing up.

Tuesday afternoon Abby was sitting for the three younger boys. In the late afternoon, Ben had returned home and joined them for a pick-up football game.

"Hoik!" Abby shouted to Mathew, who was holding the ball.

He tossed it to her. Then he raced down Bradford Court with his brothers.

Abby reared back to throw. "Go long!" she shouted. "Longer! Longer!"

The boys were scrambling ahead, trying to outrace each other, looking over their shoulders.

"Longer!"

They were at the end of the block now.

Abby tucked the football under her arm and yelled, "The quarterback fakes and goes for the run!"

"HEEEYYYYY!" shouted the brothers.

Abby took off. Giggling, the boys ran after her. She zigged onto the sidewalk and zagged left onto the Hobart lawn. "You'll never catch Swift-Foot Stevenson!" she crowed.

Fat chance. They surrounded her. Screaming, she disappeared under a pile of laughing Hobarts.

"Hi, guys!" chimed Jessi's voice from behind them.

Abby looked out from under the boy mound and saw Jessi jogging across the lawn. Behind Jessi were the two kids she was baby-sitting for that afternoon, nine-year-old Haley Braddock and Haley's seven-year-old brother, Matt. One of their friends, Buddy Barrett, had been dropped off at the Braddocks' and was tagging along with them.

Matt was wearing a strange pair of sunglasses. Each lens looked like a miniature comet, with a white, sparkly tail. Buddy had on a pair of antennae.

Abby cracked up. "Who are you two?"

"He's the beehive comet and I'm the creature who lives on him," Buddy explained.

"*Veehoff*," Haley corrected him.

Matt made a flying motion with his right hand and then began moving both hands in sign language. (Matt was born profoundly deaf, which means he can't hear even the slightest sound.)

"He says he was just passing by this planet and decided to stop in Stoneybrook," Haley explained.

"Yiiiiikes!" James shouted. "Here comes the comet! I'm — I'm dying!"

"Ehhhhhhh!" Buddy cried. "The comet alien gives you life, but you must be on my side!"

"Uh, very nice," Abby said. "Now, who wants to play foot — ?"

"I want to do what they're doing!" Johnny Hobart piped up. "How do you play, Buddy?"

"Well, the Veehoff Comet is attacking," Buddy explained, "and alien Veehoffs hop off to take over the world. The only people who can save the world are the Earthlings with super powers."

Ben was howling. "Nobody lives on comets! They're made of ice and rock!"

Abby let out a loud whistle. "Okay, football players to the street, comet people to Jessi!"

James hesitated, then ran off to comet land.

"I guess it's just you and me, huh, Ben?" Abby asked.

"Uh . . . later, Ab."

Zoom. It was a lost cause.

Jessi and Abby watched the war unfold. They died a few times, knocked off a couple of aliens, and before they knew it, it was growing dark.

Johnny sidled up to Abby and said, "I'm c-c-cold."

"Okay, aliens and Earthlings!" Abby called out. "Report inside the Hobart module for hot chocolate!"

Everyone ran into the house. Abby and Jessi heated up a kettle of hot water and poured nine cups of steaming hot chocolate.

As they sat around the kitchen table, crowded onto chairs and a piano bench, the sky slowly darkened.

"I think I see the comet!" Mathew bolted up from his chair and ran to the window.

"You *always* think you see it," James scoffed.

"Sit down," Ben ordered. "It's not coming for another week."

Mathew slumped back to the table. "Rats, I missed it."

"Don't worry," Haley reassured him. "We'll probably have the comet party at our house, and I'll let you use our telescope."

"Your house?" Buddy piped up. "No way!

My mom just bought a telescope, too. Ours is bigger."

"How do you know?" Haley asked.

"Well . . . we have a better view," Buddy muttered. "Our house is on a hill."

"That's not a hill!" James scoffed. "It's a bump."

"Bring both your telescopes to our house," Ben suggested. "We have the best view."

"Whoa, easy, guys," Abby said. "Talk to Kristy about this. She'll make the final decision."

"How about the old lighthouse?" Mathew asked. "We could have a spooky party and turn into bats at the stroke of midnight!"

"No way!" Buddy replied. "That place is haunted."

"I'm not allowed to stay up until midnight, anyway," James said.

Ben shrugged. "Too bad, because that's when the comet's supposed to come."

James looked horrified. "It *is*?"

"The newspaper said *between* eight and midnight," Jessi said. "By midnight it'll be barely visible."

"You know, we're lucky," Mathew spoke up. "If we were back home in Australia, we wouldn't see the Veehoff Comet."

"Maybe you should go back," Buddy said. "You might be safer there."

"Safer?" Mathew asked.

"Sure," Buddy replied. "It won't crash in Australia."

"It's going to *crash?*" Johnny said.

"Absolutely not!" Jessi replied. "We're nowhere near its path. All the newspapers and TV reports say that."

"When I went to the Museum of Natural History in New York, I saw a car that was smashed by a comet," Haley reported.

"I think that was a meteor," Jessi said.

"You know what I learned in school?" Jessi went on. "The word 'comet' comes from the Greek word for hair. The ancient people thought the comet's tail was white hair."

"Is it?" Johnny asked.

"No way!" Buddy replied. "It's made of fire and germs. In school we saw this picture of a forest — totally burned up by a comet that exploded in the air! Also, a famous astronomer says that comets sprinkle flu germs."

Mathew was on the verge of tears. "Then we'll all get sick!"

"Only if it passes too close," Buddy explained. "Of course, if it's *way* too close, we die."

"Buddy . . ." Jessi said warningly.

Haley was signing all this to Matt, who looked very skeptical.

"I heard that a comet caused Noah's flood,"

Ben said. "It killed the dinosaurs, too. You know what happens? When it passes across the sun, it cuts off all the light. The world goes dark for thirteen days, and all the plants die. Then the plant eaters die, then the meat eaters. That would be us, in modern times."

Johnny put his hands over his ears. "I'm not going to listen."

"On the thirteenth day," Ben continued, "rats run in the streets and dead people rise up from their graves and turn into ghosts and haunt the world — "

"Stop!" Johnny cried, then jumped into Abby's lap.

"Ben, if these kids can't sleep tonight, I'm telling their parents to call you," Abby said.

"Sorry," Ben replied with a shrug. "I think that last part is just a legend, anyway. Maybe only some of it is true."

Matt was now signing something furiously to Haley. He looked grim and concerned.

"Uh, Ben?" Haley asked. "Matt wants to know if it's expensive to fly to Australia."

Abby gave Jessi a Look. She had a feeling it was not going to be an easy night for anybody.

CHAPTER 7

"Hello, Baby-sitters Cl — I mean, hello!"

Duh. Wake up, Claudia.

My phone has two lives, BSC and non-BSC. When it's just my phone, which is most of the time, I pick it up like a normal person and say hello.

Sometimes I goof. Like when it's 5:10 on a Wednesday and all I can think about is that strange afternoon at the lighthouse and my older sister's clothes are all over my bed and she's laughing hysterically downstairs with a cute guy who's living in my house but has never even had the chance to lay eyes on me because I'm constantly cleaning up my older sister's stuff.

"Hi, Claudia, is Janine there?" a male voice asked. "This is Jerry."

"This isn't Janine's number!" I blurted out.

"I know, but she told me I could reach her here for a few weeks."

"Great. Maybe my whole family can use this line, and we'll cancel the other one."

"Sorry, but — "

I covered the receiver and screamed, *"Janine! It's your BOYFRIEND on MY phone!"*

The laughter stopped. Janine thumped up the stairs and into my room. "Tell him I'm not here," she whispered.

"Oh, right," I whispered back. "I'll just say I was calling to the other Janine!"

"Good point." Janine was pacing the few available square inches of the room. "Um, say you called me but I was just running out the door."

I took my hand off the receiver. "Sorry, I called her but she ran away. Out the door, I mean."

Janine was cringing.

"But — who were you talking to?" Jerry asked.

"Uh . . . Laura. She's one of our guests." I raised my voice. *"Okay, 'bye, Laura, thanks for sharing that with me!"*

"Sharing what?" Laura shouted from inside Janine's room.

"Listen, Claudia," Jerry said. "Tell Janine I just wanted to ask her about the orbital calculations we had to figure out in astro, okay?"

"Sure, Jerry, I have to go. 'Bye."

" 'Bye."

I hung up. "Are you happy now?" I asked Janine.

"What did he want?" Janine said.

"Something about calculus orbicles."

"Big help."

"Why don't you just break up with him?" I asked. "You seem much more interested in Steve."

Janine giggled. "Steve and I are just friends. So far. He's very sweet, you know. Only in school three days and he's practically the most popular guy. He's introduced me to people who never even used to look at me."

My older sister's first exposure to coolness. How did I feel about this?

Pained. Tortured. Especially after my ordeal with Laura at SMS.

"Don't tell anyone," Janine said, lowering her voice to a whisper, "but he really is going to have that Christmas party in the lighthouse. Just a few select friends, including me."

"He can't be serious! Janine, no one should go near that place!"

"It's just an old building — "

"Look, I told you about that guy who lives next door. Mr. Hatt says he's disturbed. I say, total psycho. Second, that place makes my skin crawl. Something happened there that no one is telling us about. I just know it. Look, you were seven or eight when the Hatts left

Stoneybrook. Don't you remember anything weird about it? Or any strange things that happened at the lighthouse?"

"Something happened one winter while we were on vacation," she said. "But Mom and Dad didn't know what, exactly. At least that's what they said. And people have always said the lighthouse is haunted, but that's silly."

"It's not silly!" I shot back. "I heard this voice there, a young voice — "

"Claudiaaaaa, don't be ridiculous." Janine glanced at her watch. "Oops, be back in four minutes. I have to finish helping Steve with his homework."

"Whoa, how about putting your stuff away first?" I said, picking up one of her blouses. "I'm having a meeting in a few minutes."

Janine gave me a blank look. "What meeting?"

"Uh, hello? It's Wednesday!"

"Well, I can't give up the room. I need to set up some spreadsheets on my computer."

"Janine, we agreed — "

"Okay, okay, have your meeting. Just keep it down."

"We can't have it if you're in the room!"

"Fine. Your choice." Janine darted out the door.

I was still holding the blouse. I eyed the X-Acto knife on my art table.

It was very, very tempting.

Instead, I heaped all of Janine's stuff, unfolded, in her dresser drawers. Then I reached between my mattress and box spring for a bag of mini–Milky Ways I'd hidden.

It was open. And half empty.

This was the last straw.

It was an act of war.

Before I could scream bloody murder, Kristy and Abby bounded into the room.

"Hi, Claudia the Cramped!" Abby greeted me.

"Here," I said, tossing them the half-finished bag. "We're meeting in the living room today."

"What?" Kristy said. "How — "

"All because of my sister, the genius who ate my bedroom."

Thank goodness for call forwarding. I had just signed up for it. I picked up the receiver, tapped out the numbers for my family's line, and hung up again.

On the way downstairs, I explained what had happened. Janine and Steve were in the den, so we kept our voices down. The three of us sprawled out in the living room, gabbing away. We intercepted Stacey, Jessi, Mallory, and Mary Anne as they walked in.

Kristy called the meeting to order at five-thirty. By that time, Janine had disappeared upstairs to monopolize our headquarters.

At 5:32, Dad walked in the door with Mr. Hatt. "Well, well," he said with a chuckle. "Looks like our meeting place has been taken over by baby-sitters."

"Meeting place?" I asked.

"Sorry, Claudia," Dad said. "Mr. Hatt and I are meeting with the title insurance agent here. I didn't know you needed the room."

"That's okay," I said, "we'll use the den."

We ran in there, only to find Steve and Caryn playing a video game.

"Where do we go now?" Mary Anne whispered.

"Follow me," I said.

Mom was clattering around in the kitchen, preparing some kind of fish. "Mind if we meet here?" I asked. "Dad's in the living room, Janine's in my bedroom, Caryn and Steve are in the den."

Mom shrugged. "Sure, if you don't mind the smell."

(If you saw a photo of our faces, you'd know how we felt about that.)

As we crowded bravely around the table, Kristy said, "Any new business?"

"Hello, everybodyyyy!" Mrs. Hatt sang, walking in with two bags of groceries.

Clunk. She set them down on the counter. "I'll be right back with the other bags!"

"As I was saying — " Kristy began.

Caryn rushed into the kitchen. "Yum! Did she buy any string cheese?"

Steve shuffled in after her and pulled a box of crackers out of one of the bags. "Cool," he said, tearing it open.

Laura raced downstairs and barged in. "You pigs! Can't you help put stuff away?"

Riiiiiinnnng! went the kitchen phone, over by the refrigerator.

"I'll get it!" I shouted.

But Mom was closer, so she picked up. "Hello? . . . Who? The Baby-sitters Club?"

"I put my phone on call forwarding!" I explained, winding my way around the three munching Hatts.

"One more load!" Mrs. Hatt announced, bustling in with more groceries. "Including ice cream!"

"Yesss!" Laura cried out.

This was hopeless. "I'll take the cordless phone, Mom! Come on, guys, it's too crowded in here!"

I dashed into the den, where I grabbed the cordless phone off the wall. Then I looked around for a quiet place to take the call. Only one room was available.

We all ducked into the bathroom.

"Hello, Claudia speaking," I said into the cordless phone.

My voice was echoing off the tiles. Abby

was cracking up. She pantomimed flushing the toilet, which I did not find funny.

"Hello, it's Mrs. Arnold," said the voice on the phone. "I need a sitter for next Sunday, three to five-ish?"

"Okay," I said. "I'll call you right back."

I hung up. I was now sitting on the closed-up toilet. Balancing the record book on her knees, Mary Anne was perched on the edge of the bathtub. Kristy was actually in it. Stacey and Abby were leaning against the sink, and Jessi and Mal were on the floor.

"It's the BSC," Abby said. "Bathroom-sitters Club!"

Suddenly the door swung open and Steve barged in.

He stopped short. His face instantly turned red. "Uh . . . sorry."

Zip. Out he went.

Abby exploded with laughter.

That was all it took. Forget it. We were gone. Cackling. If more floor had been available, we'd have been rolling on it.

We eventually caught our breath and returned Mrs. Arnold's call. (Abby took the job.)

Afterward Kristy said, "Let me try again. Any new business?"

"Well, maybe," Mallory said. "This is about the lighthouse."

The room fell silent.

"Claudia, I was spooked out by all that stuff you told us at Monday's meeting," Mallory went on. "So when my dad took us to the store last night, I asked him to drive by the lighthouse. As we passed, I thought I saw somebody at the door, trying to get in."

"What did you do?" I asked.

"I told Dad, and he stopped. But by the time we got out, the person was gone."

"Did you call the police?" Stacey asked.

Mallory shook her head. "No one believed me. Except Claire. She was scared out of her wits. The triplets thought the whole thing was hilarious — "

"EEEEEEAAAAGGHH!"

I nearly jumped off the toilet. The scream was Janine's.

We raced out of the bathroom. I could hear footsteps thumping all over the house.

Janine was standing in the front doorway. The door was open. Mom, Dad, and all the Hatts were gathered around her.

The day's mail was in a heap at her feet, along with an open cardboard box. Janine was holding a small, baseball-style cap in her hands.

"What's wrong?" I asked.

"I — I got an e-mail message that a disk would be arriving for me today, Express Mail," she explained. "So I went to check the mail, and this box was on the welcome mat. It was open, and this was in it."

She held out the hat. It was tattered and charred, as if someone had set it afire. Pinned to it was a piece of paper.

My heart skipped about when I saw what was on the paper — letters cut from various magazines and pasted together to form a message:

HATtS GO Home E

"Oh my lord," Stacey murmured.

Mr. Hatt took the hat and examined it. "Well, uh, someone's idea of a little joke. Sorry, Janine, I . . ."

His voice trailed off. He was looking at the mail on the floor. On one envelope was the name Hatt, written in big scrawly letters above our address.

Mr. Hatt knelt and picked it up. I glanced at the postmark: Stamford. All letters from Stoneybrook are marked that way.

As Mr. Hatt opened the envelope, a few ripped pieces of a photograph fell out.

Laura scooped them up. "It's the lighthouse!" she said.

But Mr. Hatt was looking at a sheet of paper he'd found in the envelope — with another cut-out message:

ASheS To ASHES
We aLL faLl down
we Have Not
ForgoTTeN

"What does that mean?" I asked.

Mr. Hatt swallowed. "I'm not sure."

"Is this from Mr. Langley?" Caryn asked.

"Possibly," Mr. Hatt replied. "He and I had a . . . misunderstanding years ago. And, well, he's not exactly a stable man."

Mrs. Hatt took both notes and looked them over. "I don't know, Alex," she said. "I never thought he'd be the type to do this."

"Creep," Steve muttered, ducking back toward the den.

"I hope he got it out of his system," Laura commented.

"Well," said my dad, "shall we clear the mail away? The insurance agent should be arriving any minute."

Done. Over. No one wanted to talk more about it. Everyone seemed sort of disgusted and baffled but determined to go on with the evening.

Me? I was completely freaked out.

CHAPTER 8

Wednesday

Okay, the game is afoot.
Sherlock Thomas is on the case.
(I even have a Watson in the
house, but I have NOT discussed
this with him.)

Fact: The Hatts left Stoneybrook
years ago for murky reasons.
Fact: The Hatts had to leave
Arizona, too. Why? Allegedly
because Steve, the Love of Claudia's
Life, was in some trouble at his
high school, which no one seems
to want to talk about. Fact: Old
Man Langley, who lives next to
the lighthouse, hates Mr. Hatt.
Fact: Someone knows where the
Hatts are staying and is threatening them.

77

Questions: Why did the Hatts leave Stoneybrook? Did Mr. Hatt do something wrong back then? What kind of trouble did Steve get into in his old school? Is Mr. Langley really disturbed, or does he have a reason to be ma Did he send the threatening messages? Or could it have been someone else? Are other people angry at the Hatts, too?

And what about that old lighthouse? Is it really haunted? What did Claudia hear and Mallory see?

Are the walking dead among us?

WHAT IS GOING ON HERE?

I shall begin my investigation at the Thomas/Brewer mansion...

Okay, let me make one thing clear. Kristy was absolutely wrong about Steve. Cute, yes. Love of my life, no.

Just needed to get that off my chest.

As you can see, Kristy loves to write in the the BSC mystery notebook. We all do. We go right to it whenever strange stuff starts happening in Stoneybrook. What do we write?

Clues, thoughts, theories — whatever we think might help solve the mystery.

And the sooner this one was solved, the better.

Okay, back to the mail incident.

I could barely speak. Janine was in shock. She told the BSC members to use the bedroom while she went out for a walk.

The moment we shut the door to my room, we all started talking at once.

"How can anyone be so slimy?" Abby asked.

"Maybe it's a prank," Mallory suggested.

Stacey exhaled. "Maybe it isn't."

"What do you think this . . . person will do?" Jessi asked.

"What did the Hatts do?" Abby said. "I mean, it must have been something big, to make someone so angry."

"It doesn't matter," Kristy shot back. "Anyone who has a problem with the Hatts should talk to them, face-to-face."

"Kristy's right," Stacey agreed. "We can't let Claudia's guests be threatened like this. It's just not right."

Mary Anne was sniffling. "What about C-C-Claudia? What if . . . you know?"

What if I was hurt? That's what she wanted to ask. I'd say it was a good question.

"We have to find out exactly what happened

79

back when the Hatts left Stoneybrook," Kristy declared, pacing the room. "Claud's parents don't seem to want to talk about it. Or maybe they're too embarrassed to discuss it in front of the Hatts. But a lot of our parents were here at the time. I'll ask Watson and my mom what they know. Mallory, you try your parents. Mary Anne, ask your dad to explain what he told you in the car all those years ago. I'll expect a group report by tomorrow."

"Yes, captain!" Stacey said.

"Claudia!" called my mom from downstairs. "Undo your call forwarding. You have a baby-sitting call!"

The rest of the meeting was wall-to-wall calls. I did manage to find the BSC mystery notebook, and we started writing what little we knew in it.

At six o'clock, Kristy said good-bye and raced outside with Abby. As usual, Charlie Thomas was waiting in the Junk Bucket. (That's the name of his car, and it fits.)

As Kristy slid into the backseat she exclaimed, "Charlie, *you* were here!"

"Aren't I always?" he asked, starting up the car. "You pay me, don't forget."

"No, she means in Stoneybrook, nine years ago," Abby said. "Do you know what happened at the lighthouse?"

Charlie thought for a moment as he pulled away from the curb. "Well, I was only eight. I remember an accident or something. They had to close the place down."

"What kind of accident?" Kristy pressed on. "A murder? An attack?"

"It's coming to me now," Charlie said. "It was a stormy night, and some girl — she was thirteen, I think — decided to sneak into the lighthouse with some friends. It was pitch-black, so they used matches to light their way. Everything was fine until they climbed to the top floor . . ."

Kristy and Abby were sitting forward, straining at their seat belts. "And?" Abby asked.

"A gust of wind blew out their match flames," Charlie continued. "And they were taken to the spirit world by the ghost of Christmas Past!"

"Dork," Kristy muttered, slumping into her seat.

"Charlie, this is important," Abby said. "This strange family is staying with the Kishis. The parents own the lighthouse — "

"Their name is Hatt," Kristy cut in. "And when Janine Kishi went to bring in the mail today, she found — "

"Steve Hatt!" Charlie exclaimed.

"You know him?" Kristy asked.

"Are you kidding? Party animal type. Real popular with the girls." Charlie laughed. "Sam's friends want to kill him."

"Why?" Abby asked.

"They were going to have this Christmas party, but they were too shy to ask the girls. So Steve goes ahead and says he's having a party of his own. Imagine, a new kid, and all the girls want to go to his party."

Kristy and Abby exchanged a Look. Suddenly Mr. Langley wasn't the only person angry at the Hatts . . .

Thursday

may be your wright Kristy. may be mr. Langly didnt do it. Infact, I have another idea whom mite have done it. you may not beleave it, tho . . .

If I spelled anything wrong, ignore it. You know what I meant.

It started as I was leaving school on Thursday with Laura. Her new best friend, Tonya Wright, was with us.

Tonya is in the cheerleader crowd. She's also kind of a sourpuss. As you might have guessed, Laura was very excited to be friends with her. Too excited.

"I had *sooooo* many friends in Arizona," Laura was saying. "I was, like, Miss Popularity."

"Yeah?" Tonya said. "My cousin lives in Arizona. I wish I lived there. The weather's much nicer. The people are more laid-back, too. Stoneybrook stinks."

"I know!" Laura agreed. "I hate it here. I'd give *anything* to move back!"

"Give it a chance," I said. "The people are laid-back here, too."

"Oh, right, look who's talking. Your parents won't even let you eat candy!" With a sly smile, Laura turned to Tonya. "Claudia has to hide junk food in her underwear drawer!"

Tonya howled with laughter. "Are you serious?"

"Lauraaaaa," I warned.

"One day I went into her room," Laura continued, "and she jumped on her bed, like I'd caught her in a crime. Her cheeks were all stuffed with candy like a chipmunk."

I couldn't believe this. Laura — *my* guest, the girl I was sacrificing my privacy for — was making fun of me to a total stranger!

I didn't deserve this. "See you later," I said, pushing my way through the front door.

I was furious. I stormed home. I snapped at Mr. Hatt, who was in the kitchen. I went to my room and started painting, just to calm myself down. I heard the others come home, Caryn with her mom, Janine with Steve, and Laura with her ego, but I ignored them. I just splattered jagged lines of blacks, grays, and purples on my canvas.

It didn't help. I had to face Laura.

I was pretty sure I'd heard her and Caryn in their room. I stalked across the hall. I took a deep breath, flung open her door, and said, "Laura — "

I was wrong. The room was empty.

Except for a pair of long scissors on Laura's bed. With small pieces of glossy magazine photos stuck to the blade.

Not to mention sections of headlines. Headlines with big letters, like the ones pasted to the threatening notes . . .

Saturday

Today Mr. Hatt hired Mary Anne and me to help clean out the lighthouse. We also had to look after Caryn. Laura refused to come. (you're right, Claudia, she sounds like a real pill).

Stacey and I had our eyes out for clues. We were ready for any little hint — a dropped scrap of paper, hair samples, forgotten tools. What we didn't expect to see was a message, freshly painted in blood red across the outer wall

HATTS OFF!

"Hmm, that wasn't there yesterday," Mr. Hatt said as he drove up to the lighthouse.

"Who wrote that, Daddy?" Caryn asked.

"Some prankster," Mr. Hatt replied. "Once we fix this place up, kids will leave it alone."

Mary Anne gulped. "M-m-maybe we shouldn't go in there."

"I'll go in first and look around," Mr. Hatt said, climbing out of the car.

Stacey, Mary Anne, and Caryn followed him to the front door. As Mr. Hatt pushed his key into the lock, Stacey noticed deep dents in the door, near the knob. "Did someone try to break in?" Stacey asked.

"Many times, over many years," Mr. Hatt

replied with a chuckle. "Some of these dents are full of rust. Thank goodness the locks held."

Stacey looked up. "I guess the window's too high for anyone to climb in."

"Much too high," Mr. Hatt said under his breath as he pushed the door open.

He disappeared inside. Stacey looked around nervously. An elderly couple was strolling across the narrow strip of sand, and a young man leaned against a nearby streetlight, looking out toward the water.

"The place looks fine," Mr. Hatt said. "Now, would you girls please cart down as much debris as you can from the second floor? I need to go downstairs and check the auxiliary generator."

"Sure," Mary Anne said.

"Yyyyyes!" Caryn exclaimed. "I want to go to the roof!"

"You go with her," Stacey said to Mary Anne. "I'll start cleaning up the second floor."

Mary Anne and Caryn headed for the top. Stacey climbed to the middle floor. Even in broad daylight, with the window facing south, the lighthouse was dark inside. The piles of equipment had not been moved yet, and Stacey imagined a mouse running out at any moment.

She began gathering smaller stuff into a pile — old plastic cups, broken pieces of china, boxes, and little metal doohickeys. Through the open window, the gentle lapping sound of the water began to ease her mind. She looked out at the distant gray hump of Long Island and the expanse of water, which began at the base of the lighthouse.

That was when she spotted the young man again. Moments before he had been leaning against the light pole. Now he was staring at the lighthouse intently.

Stacey moved closer to the window. The man turned nonchalantly and walked away, down the narrow strip of sand next to the dock. He stopped at a nearby jetty and sat.

A shiver ran through Stacey. The guy looked as if he were around college age. What was he doing here, all alone on a Saturday, staring at the lighthouse? Who was he?

Stacey moved in front of the window. She leaned out slightly and peered at the guy, trying to see if she could recognize anything familiar about him.

A voice behind her whispered, *"Do-o-o-on't . . ."*

Stacey spun around.

No one was there.

"Muh — Muh — " The word caught in her throat. She swallowed and tried again. *"Mary Anne, I'm coming upstairs!"*

We did it! *Saturday*
Mallory and I
found out what
happened at the
lighthouse! It was

Whoa, slow down, Jessi. Let's take it
from the top. Jessi and I decided to look
for articles about the lighthouse in the
Stoneybrook News of nine years ago. The
problem was, Claudia's mom was working
in the library, and we didn't want her to
know what we were doing.

So Claudia came
with us. She
chitchatted with
her mom while
Mallory and I
looked through
microfilm of back
issues. And voilà!
Here's a photocopy
of what we
found:

LOCAL BOY ICY VICTIM

The grim wait of an entire town has been put to an end today. Sixteen-year-old Adrian Langley, who was rescued from the icy waters of Long Island Sound three days ago, was pronounced dead at Stoneybrook Hospital today, as a result of head trauma and overexposure.

Early reports claimed that the young Mr. Langley had fallen while wandering onto thin ice near the Stoneybrook lighthouse. However, according to the coroner, his head injury was consistent with a fall of twenty to thirty feet. An inspection of the lighthouse revealed Mr. Langley's fingerprints on both floors. The window on the second floor was open, and the main door of the lighthouse was locked.

Mr. Langley was found in the water, in shock and barely breathing, by Mr. Alexander Hatt, a local businessman who owns the lighthouse. Mr. Hatt had stopped by to check the premises, he says, when he saw a bobbing motion in the water.

Mr. Hatt had no further comment. An investigation is pending.

The staff of the *Stoneybrook News* extends deepest condolences to Homer Langley for the tragic loss of his son.

CHAPTER
9

Sunday

There is only one listing for "Langley" in the Stoneybrook phone book. The address is 24 Shore Drive. The first name is Homer. Adrian must have been the son of the crazy man next door to the lighthouse.

Oops, this is the regular notebook, not the mystery notebook! Sorry, Kristy. Wasted paper, I know.

More to come later. In the other book.

Now. To the baby-sitting job. Jessi and I were with my brothers and sisters this afternoon. Today was also the day my dad decided to bring home an early "family Christmas present."

If I'd known what it would be, I'd have invited a couple more baby-sitters.

Or maybe Shelmadine Veehoff himself...

Actually, Mallory should have written *herself*. Shelmadine was a woman who lived in the late nineteenth century and had her own observatory on an island off Cape Cod. I looked it up.

Ahem.

Anyway, Mr. Pike's early present was a giant, super-fantastic telescope. He spent all of Sunday morning assembling it.

Mal told us later that her brothers and sisters were insane with excitement. When he was finished, Mr. Pike took the telescope outside. The kids practically fell over each other, following him.

By the way, for handy reference, here are the names and ages of Mal's siblings: Claire (five); Margo (seven); Nicky (eight); Vanessa (nine); and the triplets, Adam, Byron, and Jordan (ten).

Jessi arrived just as Mr. Pike was setting up the telescope on a tripod. "Cool!" she said.

"We get to look through it before the baby-sitters!" Margo cried.

"Boys before girls!" Nicky cried.

"No fair!" Vanessa squealed.

"Time out, everybody!" Mr. Pike yelled. "Mom and I have to leave for our concert. I was hoping to have time to supervise you, but I don't. So I can do one of two things. Put this back inside until I come home — "

"NO-O-O-O!" screamed the kids.

"Or trust you to take turns, treat this with respect, and listen to everything Jessi and Mal say."

"We will!" came a chorus of voices.

"Scout's honor," added Jordan.

"You're not a scout," Nicky grumbled.

"Be gentle," Mr. Pike said softly to Mallory. "It's a delicate instrument."

With that, he was off.

"Okay, line up in age order," Mallory called out. "Claire first."

Claire squealed with delight. Margo, Nicky, and Vanessa fell into line behind her.

The triplets, Adam, Byron, and Jordan, were jostling each other for position.

"I'm forty seconds younger than you," Adam said, elbowing in front of Jordan.

"Yeah, but I'm more interested in astrology," Jordan retorted.

"At least I know it's astro*nomy*," Byron said.

"So, you're still ugly," Adam snapped.

"What does that have to do with anything?" Byron asked.

"See? You admit it!"

Mallory harrumphed. "Byron . . . Adam . . . Jordan — that was your reverse order of birth."

The triplets grumbled into line. Jessi brought the picnic bench over and Claire scrambled on top of it.

"I don't see the comic," Claire said as she peered through the lens.

"Comet," Vanessa corrected her.

"It's afternoon," Nicky said. "You're just supposed to look at things around the yard up close."

Claire jumped down from the bench. "This is boring."

Margo stepped up next. "Ooooh," she said. "I see the neighbors in their underwear!"

"Let *me* see!" squealed the Peeping Pikes.

Mallory quickly yanked Margo away.

"I was just joking!" Margo said, stepping back up to the telescope.

As Margo continued her turn, Vanessa suddenly announced, "I made up a rhyme!"

"Oh, no," the triplets groaned.

Vanessa is the poet of the Pike family. I believe she even thinks in rhyme. She held up a sheet of paper and began to read:

" 'Comet, comet, in the sky,
Nice to see you, flying high!
We learned about you in our class;
Are you made of ice or gas?
You will be my very first comet . . .'

94

Vanessa paused. "Um, that's all I have so far."

"I can finish it!" Adam shouted. " 'Vanessa's poems just make me vomit!' "

Byron, Jordan, and Nicky burst out laughing and slapped high fives all around.

Vanessa was steaming. " 'If my brothers are on the playground, will you please bomb it?' " she snapped.

"This stinks!" Margo announced. "I can only see tree bark and stuff."

"Well, just wait until the night of the comet," Vanessa said as she stepped up to the telescope. "You'll be glad we have this."

"What's so special about a dumb comet, anyway?" Jordan complained. "I've seen a million of them."

"When?" Vanessa asked.

"In the summer," Jordan replied. "At night."

"Those are shooting stars, oatmeal brain," Adam said. "They're different."

"How?" Jordan asked.

"They're, uh, smaller," Adam fumbled. "And they're not named after people. You never heard of the Veehoff Shooting Star, right?"

"Veehoff was the name of a person?" Nicky asked. "Like, Veehoff Jones?"

"It was the name of the astronomer who discovered the comet, almost a hundred years ago," Mallory said. "Shelmadine Veehoff."

The kids cracked up. *"Shelmadine?"* Margo cried out.

"Oh my darlin', oh my darlin', oh my daaaarlin' Shelmadiiiiine . . ." Jordan warbled.

"Haley had a comet named after her," Claire piped up. "She told me."

"That's Halley's Comet," Vanessa said. "It's named after another astronomer, not Haley Braddock."

"How do you know?" Claire retorted.

"I think astronomers are very selfish," Margo said. "They should name comets after regular people, too."

"See that?" Adam pointed to the big maple tree in the Pike yard. "From now on, that will be known as the Adam tree."

"I call the Claire picnic table!" Claire shouted.

"The Margo cloud!"

"The Nicky bush!"

"The Byron house!"

"The Jordan world!"

Vanessa turned from the telescope. "You can't name the whole world for yourself, greedy."

"Oops, I have to use the Vanessa toilet," Jordan taunted her.

Vanessa darted away from the telescope and began chasing Jordan around the yard.

"My turn!" Nicky stepped up to the lens.

"Hey, I wasn't done!" Vanessa cried.

"Too late!" Nicky said. "You forfeit!"

"Do not!" Vanessa retorted.

"If you two are going to argue, step aside," Adam said.

The kids were jostling against the telescope, pushing each other.

"Hold it!" Mallory shouted. "Anyone who's ready can go inside for a Jessi and Mal snack!"

"YEEEEAAAAA!"

Instant Pike stampede.

"You go ahead and look through the telescope first," Mal whispered to Jessi. "We'll exchange places after I pour the milk."

Pretty clever, huh?

Once a good baby-sitter, always a good baby-sitter.

CHAPTER 10

"Weeeee three kiiiings of Ooooorient aaaare . . ." blasted the tinny speakers of Janine's computer.

I was trying to concentrate on a Nancy Drew novel. In about ten minutes I was supposed to leave for the lighthouse with Mr. Hatt. We were going to meet Kristy, Stacey, and Abby there.

Today, Sunday, was the Painting of the Stoneybrook Lighthouse. It was a gorgeous day, warm for December, and Mr. Hatt wanted to take advantage of the weather.

Why was I reading? To relax myself. The recent developments in the lighthouse mystery had totally blown me away. I'd hardly slept the night before. I kept dreaming that I was being chased through the lighthouse by a ghost in tatters and chains.

I tried hard not to think about the ghost. It was a figment of my imagination. It had to be.

I didn't want to be distracted from the *real* mystery.

Who had written that message on the lighthouse wall? The man who was staring at the lighthouse? Who was he? According to Stacey's description, he was too old to be a friend of the Hatt kids, too young to have known Mr. and Mrs. Hatt.

All night long, my mind tossed around theories about the culprit:

— It was the guy Stacey saw, and he was a friend of Laura's. After all, she was the one who didn't want her family to settle in Stoneybrook — and enjoyed working with scissors and magazines!

— The same guy, but he was a friend of Steve's. Another specialist in trouble-making.

— It was Laura herself.

— Steve himself.

— Mr. Hatt.

Aaaaagh. How could I possibly sleep knowing I might be living in a house full of criminals?

Maybe I wasn't, though. Maybe the bad guy was part of the Langley family. A cousin or something.

That was another weird thing. According to the newspaper, Mr. Hatt had pulled Adrian

Langley from the water. He'd tried to rescue Adrian. So why did Mr. Langley hate Mr. Hatt so much?

Nothing made sense. And now, on top of it all, I had to deal with Janine's Computer Concert.

"Could you turn that down, please?" I asked.

"Pretty good sound, huh?" Janine replied, ignoring my request. "It's a new music CD-ROM. It has classical, rock, Christmas carols — "

Christmas?

Oh, groan. Poor old Christmas. I'd been concentrating on the Hatts and the lighthouse, and the holiday season was whizzing by.

I counted slowly in my head. "Oh my lord, only nine more days until Christmas."

"Ten," Janine said. "You're slipping."

"I haven't done any shopping! Everything's been so crazy around here. What am I going to do?"

"Go with the Hatts later on," Janine suggested. "During Phase Two."

"Huh?"

"Earth to Claudia. While you and your friends are working at the lighthouse, Mrs. Hatt and her offspring will be shopping for Mr. Hatt at the mall. Then, when they're through, Mrs. Hatt is going to trade places with her husband at the lighthouse, and he'll take the kids shopping for her. You can go with them. QED. So relax."

"QED?"

"*Quod erat demonstrandum,*" Janine explained. "Also known as *quite easily done.*"

"It's all Greek to me," I muttered.

"Latin," Janine corrected me.

"Why aren't you with them, instead of here, making me feel stupid?"

"I've done most of my shopping." Janine smiled. "At least for the important gifts."

"Like mine?" I said slyly. "Oh, and Jerry's, of course."

Janine's smile disappeared. "Jerry who?"

"Ooops. Are you two fighting again? Is that why he hasn't called the last few days?"

Janine sat at her computer and turned off the music. As she clicked her mouse, she said, "Actually, I finally told him about Steve."

"Told him *what* about Steve?"

Janine was blushing. "Please, Claudia. *You* know."

Huh? What was going on here? Was she talking about the same Steve I knew? The Steve who hadn't said more than three sentences all week?

Were he and Janine having a . . . a *thing?*

Impossible. Ridiculous.

I wanted to pull her hair out.

I calmly placed my Nancy Drew book in my pillowcase. I put on a pair of thick winter socks. "See you," I said as I left.

I didn't stick my tongue out at her until I was out the door.

Janine. Caught between two suitors. The thought was too much to bear. I pictured Jerry and Steve, like two knights, dueling it out for fair Janine's hand.

As I reached the top of the stairs, I realized something awful.

What if Jerry were really angry at Janine? He wouldn't dare try to pick a fight with Steve. At least not face-to-face. But he *might* try something sneaky. Underhanded. Something that involved words, not fists.

Something like a threatening letter, maybe.

On the ride to the lighthouse, my mind was doing jumping jacks.

Jerry? Quiet Jerry Michaels, a stalker? Maybe he was the voice in the lighthouse. In movies, guys like Jerry always have secret evils lurking within. You never know.

I glanced at Mr. Hatt. He seemed to be in a great mood. (I would be, too, if I knew my whole family had gone shopping for me.) He blasted holiday music over the car radio and hummed along tunelessly.

We picked up Stacey first. She swept

through her front door, wearing a black cashmere coat with a silk scarf.

Me? I had on my mom's old Hollofil vest over an old acrylic sweater.

"Oh, is this going to be messy?" Stacey asked.

Fashion definitely had to take a backseat today. I set Stacey straight. She ran back inside and changed into something a little more funky.

Next stop, the Brewer/Thomas mansion, where Kristy and Abby were waiting.

"I have a slight allergy to paint," was the first thing Abby said. "I have to be in a well-ventilated place."

"Is outdoors all right?" Mr. Hatt said with a grin. "We'll do some scraping first, then put on a coat of primer if we have time."

When we reached the lighthouse, Mr. Hatt unlocked the door and disappeared inside. He came back out with an old radio and a handful of metal scrapers.

We began peeling all the old paint off the sides, to the sounds of holiday Muzak.

"He's fixing the house, and scraping it twice," Abby sang. "Scaring away the goblins and mice. Santa Claus is cominnnnnn' to town!"

We spread out, north, east, south, and west. I had the side closest to the house next door.

The side with the message HATTS OFF.

As I was working on the second "T," I spotted a movement behind me to my right.

I turned around. Mr. Langley was leaning over his fence, glaring at me.

When our eyes met, he began walking toward a pickup truck in his driveway.

What was *that* all about? Was he admiring my work — or angry that I was erasing his?

I sidled around the lighthouse nonchalantly, trying to whistle along with the radio.

I ran into Kristy first. "He's there!" I whispered. "Mr. Langley!"

Kristy turned and let out a shrill whistle.

I cringed. "Don't do that!"

Abby and Stacey came running. I shushed them and whispered, "Where's Mr. Hatt?"

"In the basement," Stacey replied. "Some problem with the generator."

I led them all slowly around the lighthouse. The hood of Mr. Langley's pickup was open, and he was fiddling around with the engine.

We ducked out of sight.

"I say we talk to him," Kristy said.

"Go for it," Abby agreed.

"Are you crazy?" I asked.

"Excuse me, sir?" Kristy called out, walking toward the house.

I thought I was going to die.

Mr. Langley poked his head out from under the hood. He shuffled toward us. "Yeah?"

"I hope you don't mind talking about this, but we were, uh, doing research for a historical project about the lighthouse, and we read about — well, the tragedy."

Mr. Langley just stared at her.

"Anyway, we're really sorry about what happened to your son, sir," Kristy went on. "I know you may not want to talk about it. We realize it was a horrible time — "

"Hatt talk about it to you?" Mr. Langley snapped.

I shook my head. "No."

An angry smile played across Mr. Langley's face. "Sure he didn't. Wouldn't want to admit what he did, would he?"

Kristy nodded. "We read about the rescue. It must have been — "

"Rescue?" Mr. Langley laughed. "You didn't read all the articles. You didn't read that he locked the place up with Adrian inside. Oh, sure, it was a mistake, people said. He didn't check inside enough before he closed up that night. Besides, they all said, Adrian could have slept the night and waited. He didn't have to jump. They didn't know my son had bad claustrophobia. But Hatt did, you can be sure of that."

I could feel my heart sinking. But the story

didn't make sense. "Why was Adrian in there?" I asked.

"Does it matter?" Mr. Langley shot back.

"I — I just can't believe anyone would do such an awful thing," I said.

"Tell that to Alex Hatt," Mr. Langley grunted. "Ask him about the fight he had with Homer Langley over the lighthouse property. The property that was deeded to my grandfather years ago and passed down to me, before a certain Alex Hatt illegally took it over. Ask him about the fight I put up. And about the high-priced lawyers he hired to beat down a working stiff like me. I wasn't afraid of the lawyers, no, ma'am. And Hatt knew it. He knew there was only one way to intimidate me — "

"Pop? What are you doing out there?"

A boy, high school age, was leaning out the front door.

"Just talking to these girls about Alex Hatt," Mr. Langley replied. Then he turned back to us and said softly, "Paulie was only eight at the time. He took his brother's death the hardest of all."

The boy stormed out of the house. "Don't talk about that animal, Pop," he said, grabbing his father by the arm. "Who are you kids, anyway?"

"W-w-we're helping the H-Hatts," I stammered.

Paul's eyes narrowed. When he spoke, his face reddened and the veins in his neck stood out. "The only good Hatt," he said, "is a dead Hatt."

They turned and walked to the pickup. Mr. Langley slammed down the hood. Then they climbed in, and the truck squealed away from the curb.

My teeth were chattering as we walked back toward the lighthouse.

Honk! Honnnnnk!

Mrs. Hatt's car was just pulling up. "Time to switch shoppers!" she called out cheerily.

"I'll guh — " My heart was stuck in my throat. I swallowed. "I'll get him."

I ran into the lighthouse and climbed downstairs. From outside, I could hear Stacey talking to Mrs. Hatt. Kristy and Abby stayed on the first floor and whispered a mile a minute.

Mr. Hatt was downstairs, working on an old machine. "Mr. Hatt?" I said meekly.

"Huh?" He spun around, wild-eyed. I froze.

A murderer. Adrian Langley's murderer.

I was alone with him.

"You startled me," Mr. Hatt said with a laugh.

"It's your life — I mean, *wife* — " I blathered.

"Oh! Thanks. Are you coming with me?"

"No!" I blurted out. "I mean, I think I'll do my shopping tonight."

Mr. Hatt shrugged. "Okay."

As he walked upstairs, my heart slowed down. I slumped against the wall.

I almost didn't notice the little piece of paper. It was neatly folded, gray with dust, sticking out of a piece of broken linoleum tile against the wall.

Litter. I picked it up and started to stuff it in my pocket. But I noticed handwriting on it.

I opened it up and read:

If you last the night in the lighthouse, you will be one of us.

Fred

"*No . . . NO-O-O-O-O!*" a muffled voice called out.

A cold blast of wind ruffled the note in my hand.

"*Abby?*" I shouted. "*Kristy?*"

They appeared at the top of the stairs. "Yeah?"

"Are you trying to scare me?" I asked.

Abby gave me a baffled look. "Do we need to?"

I shook it off. The voice was probably in my head.

But the wind wasn't.

And neither was the note.

CHAPTER 11

"Claudia, be careful!" Laura grabbed me by the arm and pulled me back onto the curb.

HOONNNNNK! A car whooshed by, swerving toward the other side of the road.

"Oh!" I caught my breath. "Thanks."

"Claudia, what's with you? You've been, like, in a fog all day long."

"Sorry, Laura, just . . . um, tired, I guess."

Okay, I lied. But what was I going to tell her? *I haven't trusted you ever since I found those scissors?* Or *Laura, I think your father might be a murderer?* Or *Stacey and I are hearing voices in the lighthouse?*

As it was, I could barely put a sentence together. I was obsessed with the weird note I'd found in the lighthouse on Sunday. I had been looking at it all day in school, trying to figure out what it meant. Abby, Kristy, and Stacey hadn't a clue about the meaning. Neither had the rest of my BSC friends, when I'd shown the note to them.

"I am soooo mad at Steve," Laura was saying, as we approached my house.

"Why?" I asked.

"Because he's a creep. He invited all these kids to the Christmas party in the lighthouse, but would he ask his own sister? Nooooo."

"Don't worry. Your parents wouldn't let him have it there."

"They did let him!" Laura replied. "Didn't you hear my dad give him permission this morning?"

"Well, there was a lot going on . . ."

I pushed open the front door. Caryn was already home, sitting on the sofa with her mom and dad. They were hunched over the coffee table, looking at a sheet of paper.

"Hi!" I called out.

From the grim looks on their faces and the pile of unopened mail on the floor, I had a feeling something bad had happened.

"Another letter?" Laura asked.

Mrs. Hatt nodded grimly and held it out:

You will pay!

"What does it mean?" Caryn asked.

"I don't know, sweetheart," Mrs. Hatt said. "But the joke is growing stale."

I cast a sideways glance at Laura. She turned and stormed into the kitchen. "Some joke," she grumbled.

Caryn looked on the verge of tears.

Okay, so maybe the scissors and cut-up paper in their room was just a coincidence. Either that, or Laura was a great actress.

Well, if she thought she could scare her mom into leaving Stoneybrook, the plan didn't seem to be working. Mrs. Hatt looked strong as a rock.

I sat on the sofa next to Caryn. As I was looking over the note, Janine and Steve walked in the front door.

Right away, Steve took the letter from my hand. "Hey, cool! More crank mail! I can put these on the wall for the party."

"That's the holiday spirit," Laura called from the kitchen.

"Steven, *really*," Mrs. Hatt said.

Laughing, Steve dropped the note on the coffee table. Mrs. Hatt and Caryn were now opening the other mail, so I grabbed the note and sneaked into the kitchen. "Laura?" I said.

Laura was snacking on some Triscuits. "What?"

I braced myself. "The other day, when I

went into your room to look for you, I saw — "

"You went into my room without asking?"

"Ohhhh, no!" shouted Janine. "Help!"

I darted back into the living room. Janine was holding back the curtains, peeking outside.

"What happened?" I asked.

"It's Jerry the Jerk!" she said, running for the stairs. "Tell him I'm not here. Tell him I'm in Siberia on vacation."

"Don't forget I have a meeting today!" I shouted after her.

WHAM! went my bedroom door.

Ding-dong!

Steve strode to the front door and pulled it open. "Yeah?" he grunted.

You should have seen the look on Jerry's face. If he were a cat, he would have hissed. "Is Janine home?"

"She's in Liberia," Steve said.

*"Si*beria," I corrected him. "And she's not there, anyway. Really. She's just busy, Jerry."

Jerry's eyes were still riveted on Steve. "I just want to talk to her for a minute."

"Okay by me," Steve said with an amused expression.

"I don't think so, Jerry," I said.

"Well, then, just give her this, okay?" Jerry handed me a letter. "It's very important, and very private."

Jerry glared at Steve again, then turned to leave.

"What's his problem?" Steve said as he shut the door.

"You," I mumbled under my breath.

I ran the letter upstairs, into my room. "Special delivery!"

"Is he still here?" Janine asked.

"No, but he left a love message."

I handed the letter to her and watched her open it. She pulled out a few sheets of yellow legal paper.

"No magazine cutouts?" I asked.

"Do you *mind?*" Janine snapped.

I sat at my art desk and pulled out the lighthouse note from my bag.

The crude little drawing at the bottom looked familiar, but I couldn't figure out why. I spread the note out flat and sketched the little face myself. I tried to fill in details, imagining what it might be based on.

My third attempt looked like this:

As I drew it, I noticed Janine looking over my shoulder. "Do *you* mind?" I asked.

"That's really quite a good likeness," Janine remarked.

"Do you know what it is?"

Janine nodded. "I see it every day. It's the gargoyle over the high school entrance."

Thump. That was my heart. "It is?"

"Of course, most gargoyles are based on a few basic patterns," Janine went on. "So this one could be from anywhere."

"ANYBODY SEEN MY CASHMERE SWEAT-ER?" Laura called out at the top of her lungs.

"No-o-o-o!" yelled Steve in a mock-female voice from downstairs.

"JERK!" she shouted back.

"WHERE DID YOU WEAR IT LAST?" Mrs. Hatt asked.

Clump-clump-clump-clump went Laura's footsteps up the stairs. "I think Janine had it."

Smack! went my bedroom door as Laura pushed it open. "Do you?" she asked Janine.

"Come in, the door's open," Janine said sarcastically. "And no, I don't have yours, but I own a similar one." She dug into what was once *my* closet and pulled out a grayish cardigan.

"Not my style," Laura said flatly.

A burning smell wafted up from downstairs. An alarm was beeping manically. I ran into the hall and yelled, "Is something on the — "

"WHO-O-O-OA!" came Steve's voice.

"Steven Hatt, haven't I always told you to keep newspapers away from the top of the stove?" Mrs. Hatt yelled.

"Helloooo, I'm home!" sang my mom from the front hallway. "What's that smell?"

Laura and Caryn were running downstairs at top speed.

I could hear clattering noises and splashing water in the kitchen. Steve was whooping loudly, as if the whole thing were a hilarious joke.

Janine turned to me with a weary look. "I don't know about you, but I can't wait until they leave."

For once, my sister and I were in full agreement.

By BSC meeting time, the fire was out and the house had calmed down.

Our first order of business was the comet party. Mary Anne told us her dad had agreed to be on hand, to supervise and to drive home anyone who didn't have a ride.

After a phone call came in, I passed the latest letter to the Hatts around the room, along with my drawing.

"The gargoyle face does look familiar," Stacey said.

Kristy nodded. "Sort of like my brother Charlie just after he wakes up."

"We'll have to scout the high school tomorrow," Abby suggested. "Check out the statue."

Jessi leaped to her feet. "I've got it!" she cried, holding up the crank letter. "Okay, clue number one — the postmark says Stamford, just like the other, so the notes are probably local. Clue number two — look at the cutouts. Who would have a magazine like this in the house?"

We all leaned forward. Most of the letters in the message were pretty average-looking. But a couple of them caught my eye. The fonts were wild, colorful. One of the letters was superimposed on the face of a rock singer. Another looked as if it had been cut from an ad for a video game.

"Someone young!" I exclaimed.

"Or the parents of someone young," Kristy added.

"Terrific," Abby said. "That narrows the suspects to . . . Mr. Langley, his son, the guy who was staring at the lighthouse, Laura, Steve, and Jerry."

Duh.

It felt as if all the air had been let out of the room.

We were still at square one.

CHAPTER 12

Tuesday

Pneumonia.
A broken zipper.
World hunger.
Bad grades.
Stomachaches.
Yucky dinners.
Hard homework.
Global warming.
A visit from Aunt Norma, who has
 bad breath.

Pimples.
 Is there anything the Veehoff
Comet is not blamed for?
 Honestly, I thought the BSC comet
party would be easy. I didn't think
we'd be dealing with the Stoneybrook Superstition Society!

Charlotte Johanssen was wearing a surgical mask when Stacey picked her up Tuesday night.

"What's that for?" Stacey asked.

"So I don't catch the flu," Charlotte replied.

Charlotte's mom, Dr. Johanssen, shrugged. "I tried to tell her it hasn't been proven that comets spread germs, but she didn't want to take chances."

Stacey tried not to laugh. Charlotte is one of the smartest and most mature eight-year-olds any of us has ever met. But hey, a kid is a kid.

Stacey's job was to round up Charlotte and the Braddock kids for the Great and Fabulous Once-in-a-Lifetime Baby-sitters Club Comet-Watching Festival. (That name was Kristy's idea, of course.)

Haley and Matt answered their door in vampire costumes over their down coats. "Boo-ah-hah-hah-hah!"

"Uh, isn't it the wrong time of year?" Stacey remarked.

"This is to ward off the ghosts," Haley explained.

Charlotte giggled. "That's silly," she said, her voice muffled by the mask.

Together they walked to Mary Anne's house. Why did we pick her house for the gala event?

Because we needed someplace big and dark. Big, to fit all the kids. Dark, because street light makes it harder to see stars in the sky. And Mary Anne's yard happens to be pretty far from any street lamps.

When Stacey and Charlotte arrived at the party, it was seven o'clock and pretty dark already. A few floodlights were on, illuminating a yard full of Pikes.

"Greetings!" Mary Anne's dad called out. "Mallory's near the barn, setting up her telescope."

Charlotte ran off to see. But Stacey couldn't take her eyes off the Pike kids. They were putting up a tent and covering it with tinfoil.

"Making a spaceship?" Stacey asked.

Adam rolled his eyes. "No, a gamma ray protector!"

"Who's Grandma Ray?" Claire Pike asked.

Well, the triplets thought that was hilarious. They fell on the ground, laughing.

"Silly-billy-goo-goo," Claire muttered and stormed away.

She was almost knocked over by Buddy Barrett. He was running across the yard, wearing a pair of mirrored sunglasses. "What's so funn — " he managed to say before falling flat on his face.

Behind him were Jessi and her eight-year-old sister, Becca, plus three of Buddy's siblings: Taylor DeWitt (who's six), Lindsey DeWitt (eight), and Suzi Barrett (five). All three of them wore mirrored sunglasses, too.

"Don't tell me," Stacey said. "To ward off the glare?"

Lindsey shook her head. "To reflect back the hypnotic rays."

"Oh."

Next came Logan Bruno with the Hobart kids, lugging a huge cooler. "Full of fruits and vegetables," Mathew Hobart explained. "In case the comet dust kills all the plants."

Where was I during all this? At the drugstore with Marilyn and Carolyn Arnold, twin eight-year-old BSC charges. I was helping them buy hairspray.

As the cashier rang up their purchase, I looked at my watch. "We're running late, you two. I don't understand why you couldn't do this another day."

"Claudiaaaaaa," Marilyn said. "It's for the comet!"

"The comet won't care what you look like," I informed her.

"Don't you know what *comet* means?" Carolyn asked. "It's Greek for hair. That's what the tail of the comet is made of. What if it sweeps across the earth and whips around everybody?"

"With the hairspray, we can stiffen it before it gets to us," Marilyn elaborated.

The cashier looked totally bewildered. I think she believed them.

Armed and ready, we hiked to the parking lot, where Mrs. Arnold was waiting in her car.

We arrived at Mary Anne's house to find a big argument raging.

"Ben, you're just trying to scare us!" Haley said.

"I'm only telling you what I read!" Ben retorted. "In the olden days, people always knew that when a comet came, it meant someone was going to get sick and die."

"I have a sniffle," Suzi said, with a frightened look in her eyes.

"That doesn't count as sick," Buddy reassured her. "Nobody here is sick. Just Ben — sick in the head."

"I think I need a scarf," Claire whimpered.

Matt signed something to Haley.

"Matt says he has a sore throat," Haley relayed to us.

"Oh, noooo!" Margo said.

With a wheeze and a cough, the Junk Bucket pulled up. Kristy and Abby climbed out, shouting hellos.

"Hi!" James Hobart greeted Kristy. "Where's David Michael?"

"Home," Kristy replied. "He has the flu."

Claire Pike burst into tears.

Suzi and Margo joined her. Taylor was teetering dangerously on the verge.

"I liked him," Buddy said sadly.

The gathering suddenly looked like a funeral.

"Was it something we said?" Abby asked.

Stacey explained everything. Right away we could all see the wheels turning in Kristy's head.

"Okay, kid huddle!" Kristy called out.

The BSC to the rescue. We herded the kids around Kristy.

"One day," she said, "I noticed that if I ate waffles in the morning, it became dark at night."

Johnny Hobart burst out giggling. "That's silly!"

"Really?" Kristy asked. "What would happen if I ate meatloaf?"

"You'd have a tummyache," Claire replied.

"It would still get dark at night!" Vanessa spoke up.

"Well, maybe. But I always open my locker with my right hand on Friday afternoons, because whenever I do that, we have no school the next day!"

"No-o-o-o-o!" squealed the little kids.

"Just because you *do* those things," Marilyn called out, "doesn't mean they make the other stuff happen!"

"In ancient times," Kristy said, "people thought that if you killed animals, the gods would make it rain."

"They were just as silly as you!" Taylor exclaimed.

"They also thought that if a comet came, someone would grow very ill," Kristy went on.

"People get sick whether a comet comes or not!" Mathew shouted.

"Precisely." Kristy smiled.

Taylor, Suzi, Claire, and Margo dried their tears.

Thank you, Kristy the Wise.

Mary Anne's dad poked his head out the back door.

"Should be here any minute, guys! Should I cut the lights?"

"Yeaaaa!" came the response.

At exactly 8:07, a small pinprick of light appeared in the northeast. It grew slowly, until it looked like a tiny streak of sky-writing.

In the telescope it looked enormous. I don't know why, but it brought tears to my eyes.

Not all the kids were so impressed. "I like the Fourth of July better," was Buddy's comment.

I took a quick look around as Veehoff streaked across the sky. Mary Anne's yard was littered with dropped sunglasses, cans of hairspray, and a surgical mask that blew gently into the entrance flap of an empty, foil-covered tent.

CHAPTER 13

"Revolting," Stacey said.

"Disgusting," Kristy commented.

"What a hunk," Abby remarked.

I looked closely at the drawing I'd found in the lighthouse. "It's definitely the same face."

It was Wednesday afternoon. Mary Anne was at a sitting job, but the rest of us had walked to Stoneybrook High School. Over our heads, above the front doors, a small statue of a hideous, grinning monster leered down at us.

Why does SHS have a gargoyle over its entrance? I have no idea. It sure didn't fit the architecture. Maybe the builder had a spare one lying around.

We'd arrived at the school just after the last-period bell (SHS classes end a half hour after SMS's). Crowds of high school kids were pouring out the front door, but we hardly noticed them.

"I mean, even though we know where the

face came from," I went on, "what good does it do?"

"It narrows the suspects to high school kids," Stacey said.

"Or teachers," Kristy added.

"Do you think Mr. Langley was ever a teacher?" I asked.

"He's mean enough," Abby replied.

"Hi, girls!" a voice piped up. "Gargoyle watchers, huh?"

Mrs. Martinez, an SHS teacher who's also a BSC client, was walking toward us. "Fred's fans are getting younger every year," she went on with a smile.

I felt as if someone had thrown a bucket of ice water in my face. "Did you say *Fred?*"

"That's what the kids have always called that gargoyle, even back when I was a student," Mrs. Martinez replied. "You never heard of Fred parties?"

Kristy, Abby, Stacey, and I all exchanged a Look. "No," I said.

"It was a yearly high school tradition," Mrs. Martinez explained. "We used to dress up as him . . . er, *it*."

"*That's* why Charlie looks the way he does," Kristy said.

Mrs. Martinez laughed. "I'm afraid the tradition is long gone. The administration became anti-Fred."

"Too many parties?" I asked.

"No, the wrong spirit," Mrs. Martinez replied. "About eight or nine years ago, a small group of students — almost a gang, I guess — adopted Fred as its symbol. Biiiig mistake."

Before I could ask another question, Charlie Thomas walked out the door and came gallumphing over to us, shouting, "If you think I'm going to give you a ride home, Kristy, forget it! I have to do shopping for Steve's Christmas party."

"Fine," Kristy snapped. "Go ahead. 'Bye!"

Mrs. Martinez was looking at her watch. "Oops, I have to pick up Luke from gymnastics. See you!"

As she ran off, Kristy scowled at her brother. "You spoiled everything!"

"Huh?" Charlie said.

Stacey suddenly jabbed me in the side. "Claudia, look who's coming!"

We all glanced toward the door again. Heading our way was Paul Langley. " 'S'up, Charlie?" he mumbled.

"Hey, Pablo," Charlie mumbled back.

Paul did a double take. "Hey, you know these girls?"

"That one's my sister," Charlie replied, jerking his thumb toward Kristy.

Paul gave us a little half smile. "You look alike."

"Thanks a lot," Charlie said.

"Paul?" Kristy spoke up. "I need to ask you a question."

Paul glared at her as if she were a mosquito on his arm.

"It's about your brother, Adrian," Kristy pressed on.

Paul's face became rock-hard. He didn't say a word.

"Kristyyyy," I whispered.

Leave it to Loudmouth Kristy. Just what we needed, a big fight. I could see the local headline now: RUMBLE AT SHS! MIDDLE SCHOOL STUDENTS SUSPENDED FROM HIGH SCHOOL BEFORE THEY ENROLL.

"Did he belong to any high school gangs?" Kristy barreled on. "You know, like that . . . Fred gang?"

"How would I know?" Paul grumbled. "I was just a kid. Why is this your business?"

"She's just naturally nosy," Charlie said.

"That's not true!" I blurted out. "Look, I found something that may have to do with the way Adrian died."

I pulled the letter from my pack and handed it to him.

Paul's face went white. His hand was shaking as he took the letter and read it. "Where'd you get this?"

"In the lighthouse," I replied.

"This face on the bottom," Paul said. "I remember Adrian once drew it for me."

"Is this his handwriting?" Stacey asked.

Paul shrugged. "I don't know. I have some of his stuff at home."

"Can we see it?" Kristy asked.

I thought Paul would blow up at her. Instead, he handed me the note and nodded. "I guess."

"I'll drop you all off, if you hurry," Charlie volunteered.

I glanced at Abby and Stacey. They looked the way I felt — absolutely horrified about being alone with Paul in his house.

"*Vámonos*," said Paul as he walked toward the parking lot.

Kristy and Charlie followed close behind.

What else could Mary Anne, Stacey, and I do? We couldn't let Kristy go alone.

My knees were shaking as we headed for the Junk Bucket.

Mr. Langley was gone when we arrived at Paul's house. (Thank goodness.) Paul unlocked the front door and led us into a small bedroom in the back. Through the closed window we could hear the Junk Bucket wheezing down the road.

On the walls were baseball team photos, a couple of perfect attendance certificates, and yellowing posters from rock groups I hadn't heard about in years.

"Pop left the room exactly the same," Paul said softly.

He opened a drawer in Adrian's old desk and pulled out a thick scrapbook. As he paged through it, a few loose things fell out: a dried leaf, a few ticket stubs, a drawing . . .

"Here it is." He held out the scrapbook, opened to a fading color photograph of a group of kids standing in front of SHS.

We all gathered around. The four boys in the photo were totally unfamiliar. One of them was mugging for the camera, grinning evilly. The others were frowning, and two were holding lit cigarettes.

From the angle, I could tell the photographer must have been kneeling or lying down. The boys were all looking down, and the gargoyle's head was peeking out from above them.

"Which one is Adrian?" I asked.

"Guys, look!" screamed Stacey from Adrian's bedroom window.

Kristy, Abby, Paul, and I rushed to her side.

Next door, smoke was billowing out through the lighthouse window.

"What the — " Paul murmured.

"Where's your phone?" I asked.

"In the kitchen!" Paul said.

I stuffed the photo into my coat pocket and followed Paul into the kitchen. Grabbing the receiver, I dialed 911 and asked for help. Then I dialed my own number.

"Hello?" Janine answered.

"Janine, tell Mr. Hatt that the lighthouse is on fire!" I shouted. *"I already called nine-one-one!"*

"Hatt?" Paul grabbed the receiver from my hand and hung up the phone. "I don't want him over here!"

"He owns the place, Paul!" I said.

Kristy, Abby, and Stacey were already running out the front door. I followed close behind.

Three cars had stopped, and the passengers were watching the smoke. We could do nothing but stand and gawk with them.

But even before help arrived the smoke began to die down. It became a few long wisps that thinned out and disappeared into the air.

"Maybe it wasn't a fire," Kristy said. "Just a smoke bomb or something."

"Why would anyone do that?" Abby asked.

"A warning?" Stacey guessed.

I could see words scratched into the ground,

on a grassless patch near the lighthouse entrance.

As I approached, the message became clear:

THE PARTY'S OVER!
STAY AWAY OR ELSE!

The fire department arrived then . . . and left. And then Mr. Hatt's car screeched to a stop at the curb. He, Laura, and Steve raced toward us. They stopped short when they saw the message.

"The party . . ." Steve let out a low whistle. "Someone's trying to scare my friends and me."

"Sure looks like it," Mr. Hatt said. "And I've had just about enough of this."

"I guess Steve can't have his little party, huh?" Laura taunted.

"That's not what I said," Mr. Hatt retorted. "I will not let us be intimidated. Steve, if you want that party, you're going to have it. In fact, the bigger, the better."

"Yyyyyyyes!" Steve said.

"We'll *all* come," Mr. Hatt continued. "The whole family, the Kishis, the Baby-sitters Club — the entire town if they want!"

I thought Steve was going to die on the spot. *"Whaaaaaaat?"*

133

Mr. Hatt pulled his keys out of his pockets. "Let's check for damage."

"But Dad, this was my idea," Steve protested.

Stacey, Kristy, Abby, and I followed the Hatts to the door.

On the way, I looked around for Paul.

He was nowhere to be seen.

CHAPTER 14

"I'm worried," I said at the BSC meeting that afternoon. "Steve's party is just two days away. Whoever is behind all this lighthouse trouble is angrier than ever. He's already smoke-bombed the place. What if he attacks the party?"

"How do you know it's a he?" Mallory asked.

"I don't," I replied. "I'm so confused at this point, you could convince me *Janine* did it."

"That's it!" Abby exclaimed. "If the Hatts leave, she has her bedroom back!"

"At least we can be sure Steve didn't do anything," I said. "He wouldn't trash his own party."

"I say it's Mr. Langley," Stacey spoke up. "He thinks Mr. Hatt killed his son."

Kristy shook her head. "He doesn't seem the type to do stuff like that. He's so . . . plain and straightforward. I think it's Paul."

"But Paul was with us when the smoke bomb went off," Stacey reminded her.

"That still leaves Laura," Mary Anne said, "and Jerry, Janine's boyfriend."

Kristy shook her head. "Not Laura. She was at the Kishis' when Claudia called, after the smoke bomb."

"I just don't know about Jerry," I said. "I mean, he *is* angry. You should have seen him looking at Steve. But would he go through all that trouble to show it?"

"People rejected in love do bizarre things," Mallory suggested.

"Yeah, but rejected by *Janine?*" I said.

"I've got it!" Abby exclaimed, jumping to her feet. "It was the ghost of Shelmadine Vee-hoff!"

"Down, girl," I said.

"If it isn't Paul, Laura, Steve, or Jerry . . . " Stacey wondered.

"Then who's doing all of this?" Kristy finished her sentence. "Who would want the Hatts out of the lighthouse?"

I drummed my fingers on my night table. Adrian Langley's photo was sitting on my dresser. Absently, I stared into the four angry, sullen faces, wondering which was Adrian, and if one of them had left that weird message in the basement.

I reread the message, which lay next to the photo: IF YOU LAST THE NIGHT IN THE LIGHT-HOUSE, YOU WILL BE ONE OF US — FRED.

Then it hit me.

I grabbed the phone book and looked up Langley.

"What are you doing?" Stacey asked as I tapped out the number.

On the second ring, Paul's voice answered. "Hello?"

"Paul, it's Claudia Kishi. I — "

"I don't have anything to say to you!" Paul snapped.

"Don't hang up! I just have one question: Which person in the photo is Adrian?"

"The photo you stole?"

"I'll bring it back. Promise. Just tell me!"

"None of them."

"None? Then why did he have it?"

"Buddies, I guess. I don't know! Why don't you ask one of them?"

Click. The phone went dead.

I slammed down the receiver. Six pairs of eyes were giving me the Big Duh.

I held up the "Fred" note in one hand and the photo in the other. "Let's say this group left this note."

Six nods.

"Adrian wasn't in the picture," I pressed on.

"Maybe he wasn't in the group at all. But we do know he was locked in the lighthouse overnight."

" 'If you last the night in the lighthouse, you will be one of us,' " Stacey read. "Oh my lord, you think the note was *for* Adrian? He wanted to be in the group, but had to go through some test first?"

"One of those guys did it?" Mary Anne asked.

"Maybe," I answered. "And maybe he's the one who's been vandalizing the lighthouse and scaring the Hatts."

"Why would he do that?" Abby asked.

I shrugged. "Maybe he's crazy. It's just a theory."

"Stacey," Kristy said, "remember the guy you saw staring at the lighthouse? Did he look like any of the gargoyle guys?"

Stacey looked closely at each face. I gazed over her shoulder.

Caucasian. Dark eyebrows. Curly brown hair. Snarly lips.

Latino. Wide-set eyes. Big shoulders.

Caucasian. Blond. The grin. A David Letterman-type gap between his front teeth.

Asian. Polynesian, maybe. A little overweight.

"I can't tell," Stacey finally said. "The guy

was wearing a hat, and he was pretty far away."

"Make copies," Kristy ordered. "We have two days to memorize these faces. Steve's Christmas party is on Friday, and we're all going. If we see one of these people between now and then, we have to recognize him right away."

"One problem, Kristy," Jessi said. "They're a lot older. If they were seventeen then, they'd be twenty-six now."

Kristy sighed. "Let's just hope they haven't changed too much."

By Friday night, every one of those faces was locked in my memory. I'd had dreams about them: The overweight Asian guy as a space invader. The gap-toothed blond guy interviewing me on TV. The dark-featured snarly guy sitting for a portrait, and morphing into the broad-shouldered Latino when I was halfway through painting him.

I was sick of them.

For the party, Steve and his friends had really decked the lighthouse, and not just with boughs of holly. A stereo system blasted rock tunes. The refrigerator was full of soda and food. The big light at the top had been fixed, and it rotated slowly, red on one side, green on the other. Strings of Christmas lights wound down from the roof in a widening spiral.

The place was packed. People were spilling out onto the lawn, dancing on the sand, walking down the dock. Steve's invitation list must have included half the school. (It's amazing how many friends you have when you throw a party.)

"Ho ho ho! Have a cup of Christmas cheer!" boomed Mr. Hatt. Wearing a rumpled Santa hat, he served punch and soft drinks from a table on the ground floor. Mrs. Hatt was pouring some munchies into bowls. (Steve, as you can imagine, looked extremely embarrassed. I don't think this was the kind of party he'd had in mind.)

Behind Mr. and Mrs. Hatt a sign hung across the spiral staircase: GROUND FLOOR AND BASEMENT ONLY, PLEASE. (I guess Mr. Hatt didn't want to risk any more accidents.)

I mingled for awhile, but the party wasn't much fun. Janine was busy following Steve around, Laura and Caryn were helping their dad and mom, and I didn't know most of the kids there.

Besides, my friends and I were on the lookout. Every fifteen minutes we met outside the lighthouse for updates.

"Anything suspicious?" Kristy asked at our 8:15 gathering.

"I saw someone put a can of soda in his inside coat pocket," Abby reported.

"Big help," I replied.

Stacey sighed. "I keep thinking I see people from that photo. A lot of these guests look like the faces."

"No messages?" I asked. "No words in the dirt? No moaning ghosts?"

Everyone shook her head.

"Okay, report back in fifteen," Kristy said.

As my friends wandered into the crowd, Janine ran to me. She looked angry and preoccupied. "Have you seen the S Man?"

"The S Man?" I repeated. "Is that Steve?"

"I find the name puerile, too," Janine replied. "Just like him."

Out of the corner of my eye, I spotted Steve walking toward the beach, arm-in-arm with a red-haired girl. "Uh, there he is," I said.

As Janine stared at him, the lighthouse searchlight washed her face red, then green. My heart went out to her. Suddenly I felt guilty for all my catty comments.

Finally, with a sad sigh, she said, "I wonder if Jerry's home."

That was when I noticed the searchlight flicker.

It was just the hint of a shadow. But it interrupted the red light that was passing across Janine's face.

I looked up. Something moved quickly across the lens.

Somebody was up there.

As Janine walked off, I darted into the lighthouse. Elbowing my way past the partygoers, I reached the spiral stairs.

I ducked under the warning sign and ran upstairs.

The second floor was totally empty. From below, the muffled beat of the stereo was shaking the floor. A string of Christmas lights hung across the newly repaired window, casting dim streaks of red, green, and orange against the dusty floor.

"He's heeeere . . ."

The voice nearly made me dive downstairs. It seemed to come from just behind my left ear.

"Hello?" I said.

No one answered.

A breathy singer from the CD. That's all it was. It had to be.

I kept climbing the spiral stairs. Above me the trapdoor opening flashed green and red from the slowly turning light.

"Anybody up there?" I called out.

I heard a thump. I stopped.

A shadow moved into the square at the top of the stairs. The shadow of a tall man.

I tried to say something, but no sound came out.

142

The red light swept across the man's face. He was blond and bearded.

"May I help you?" he said with a big smile.

My heart stopped when I saw the gap between his front teeth.

CHAPTER 15

"Who — what — you're not supposed to be up here!" I stammered.

"Oh?" He shone a flashlight in my face and I had to turn away. "Thank you for telling me. I was just . . . looking for something. Be right down."

The light flicked off. I looked up again, and he had ducked out of the circle.

I ran downstairs. Just below the second-floor landing I screamed, *"Mr. Haaaaaaaatt!"*

Some of the partygoers turned to look at me. "Can't you read the sign?" one of them said.

I pushed my way to the refreshment table. Laura and Caryn were there alone. "Where's your dad?" I demanded.

"He had to go outside," Laura replied.

Through the open doorway I could see a small crowd. Among them were all my BSC friends.

I ran out. "Mr. Hatt!"

Mary Anne was the first to see me. "Claudia, are you all right?"

"He's up there!" I blurted out. "On the top floor — the guy from the picture!"

"Which guy?" Stacey asked.

"The blond one, with the gap between his teeth!" I shot back.

"Let's get him!" Kristy said.

"No, he might be dangerous!" I began pushing into the crowd. *"Mr. Hatt!"*

"A private function?" Mr. Langley's voice thundered above the sound of the party. *"This is a disturbance of the peace!"*

I broke through to the center of the circle. There, Mr. Langley was standing face-to-face with Mr. Hatt, shouting. Paul stood behind his dad, arms folded.

"Mr. Hatt, someone's at the top of the lighthouse!" I shouted.

"Can't these kids read the sign — " Mr. Hatt began.

"It's not a kid! It's a stranger! A guy who doesn't belong here!"

That did it. Mr. Hatt broke away and ran into the lighthouse. Kristy, Abby, Stacey, Mary Anne, Jessi, Mallory, and I were right behind him.

Mr. Hatt took the steps two at a time. When he stopped at the second floor, I nearly ran into him.

Squinting into the dimly lit room, he called out, "Anyone up here?"

Kristy stepped around me and quickly scanned the area. "No one," she said.

Mr. Hatt looked upward, toward the roof. "Then he has to be there."

This time he stepped slowly.

Green . . . black . . . red . . . black . . . The searchlight turned, leaving brief gaps of darkness.

Below us, a rock ballad throbbed intensely.

Now Mr. Hatt was standing at the top step. I peered over the lip of the trapdoor.

"Hey, move up so we can see!" called Abby from behind me.

"Ssssshh," I said.

In the brief sweeps of light, I could see nothing unusual.

And then, in the shadow of the wall, something moved.

"Who are you?" Mr. Hatt called out.

He was answered by a sharp click.

The spinning light went out. The rock ballad stopped. The Christmas lights blinked off.

Loud groans wafted up from below.

"He flipped the emergency circuit breaker!" Mr. Hatt said, disappearing into the darkness.

"Be careful!" I shouted.

Kristy practically climbed over my back. I

hoisted myself onto the roof and stood up. My friends jostled by me.

"I think I saw him!" Kristy called out.

"Where?" Stacey shouted.

I banged my head on the bottom of the searchlight, which had just stopped revolving. "Yeeow!"

Click!

The lights popped back on again. Mr. Hatt was at the switch, looking around intently.

I scanned the floor for the gap-toothed man. He was nowhere.

"Who let him go downstairs?" Kristy demanded.

"No one." Mallory and Mary Anne peeked shyly over the trapdoor opening. "We were here the whole time."

"EEEEEEEAAAAGGGHHHHH!"

The scream was from outside, near the dock.

We all stood up and looked over the half wall.

I gasped.

The blond guy was climbing down the side of the lighthouse, clinging to a string of unlit Christmas lights.

I glanced backward and saw that the plug end of the lights had been tied securely around a brass hook in the wall.

"Someone stop him!" Mr. Hatt cried out.

The blond guy looked up. His eyes were wild with fear. He dug his foot into a large crack in the wall for support.

And then the wire snapped.

"NOOOOOO!" I cried.

He landed with a loud splash in the water.

We all scrambled downstairs and ran outside. The entire party was gathered at the dock now. Mr. Langley was leaning over it into the water. "Grab my hand!" he shouted.

Panting, the young man reached for him and held on. Mr. Langley yanked him up onto the grass.

The man was shivering violently.

"Paul, get a blanket from the house!" Mr. Langley shouted. "And call an ambulance!"

He and Mr. Hatt both took off their coats and put them around the young man's shoulders.

"You'll be all right," Mr. Langley said reassuringly.

"Th-th-thanks, Mr. L-L-Langley," the young man said.

Mr. Langley looked him in the eye. "Do I know you?"

"N-No."

I felt bad for the stranger. I didn't want to add to his pain. But Adrian Langley hadn't been as lucky as he. And I couldn't let him lie to Adrian's dad.

"You were in the group, weren't you?" I asked. "The group that Adrian Langley wanted to join?"

The young man looked at me, his eyes like giant snowballs.

"The group that left this note in the lighthouse." I reached into my pocket and pulled out the "Fred" message.

I could see the pulse hammering in Mr. Langley's temples. "Patrick Belknap," he murmured.

The young man nodded. "I didn't have the beard then."

"But — why — ?" Mr. Hatt stammered.

"That n-note," Patrick said, sniffling. "I left it. I was the leader of the G-Gargoyles. Adrian wanted to join. So we had to give him the t-t-test."

"What test?" Mr. Langley asked.

Patrick's voice was a pained whisper. "You had to g-go into the lighthouse and f-find the secret message. While you were looking, we l-l-locked the front door. Then, if y-you were too scared to obey — t-too scared to sp-spend the night — y-you were out of l-luck. You had to do it anyway."

Mr. Langley's face fell. He looked about ten years older. "So that was why Adrian — "

Patrick nodded. "All these y-y-years I've been trying to get in there. T-trying to find that message. I d-d-didn't want the Hatts to find it before me."

"So you sent all the threats," Kristy said.

"And planted the smoke bomb," I added.

"You were the guy I saw staring at the lighthouse while we were cleaning up!" Stacey exclaimed.

"Yes," Patrick whispered.

"You locked my son in," Mr. Langley said, his voice choked and rasping, "and Alex had nothing to do with it."

"I . . . I'm so, so sorry." Patrick broke down in tears.

Mr. Langley looked at him a good long time. I thought for sure he'd push Patrick back into the water. Or worse.

But he did nothing. A few moments later, when an ambulance roared up and a pair of paramedics led Patrick away, Mr. Langley just stood and watched.

By the curb, the entire crowd was alive with excited talk. But my friends and I stayed by the dock, along with my parents, my sister, Mr. Langley, and the Hatts.

Finally Mr. Hatt put an arm around Mr. Langley's shoulders. "I'm sorry this had to happen," he said.

Mr. Langley's eyes were moist. "I owe you, Alex. I guess we should have a nice, long talk."

"Why don't you and Paul come to our new place sometime?" Mrs. Hatt spoke up.

"New place?" my dad repeated.

Mr. Hatt smiled. "I haven't told you because I didn't want to jinx it. Just this evening we reached an agreement. The house is in move-in condition."

"Plus, the job at the insurance company looks as if it'll come through for me," Mrs. Hatt added. "We'll be up and running within a week."

I kept myself from jumping up and cheering.

"Well, we'll . . . uh, miss you," my mom said.

Just then, a voice cried out, "Hey, what happened here?"

Janine's face lit up. "Hi, Jerry!"

Jerry Michaels was bounding toward us, his face twisted with concern. He put an arm around Janine and said, "I'm glad it wasn't you."

Janine glanced at Steve with a tiny but triumphant smile. Then she and Jerry walked off, hand in hand.

And you know what? Steve actually looked angry.

Go figure.

Mr. and Mrs. Hatt were now walking across the lawn with Mr. Langley and Paul, deep in conversation. Caryn followed them, but Steve stalked away toward his friends. The rest of us stood there, a little shell-shocked, watching the partygoers say their good-byes and leave.

"I feel so sad for Mr. Langley," Laura said. "All this time I thought he was sending us those letters."

I felt sad for him, too. But at the same time, relief was washing over me. The Hatts were innocent. Mr. Hatt *had* tried to save Adrian. I wasn't in any danger at the house. "You're going to think I'm crazy," I said, "but when I saw those cut-up magazines on your bed, I thought *you* might be involved in this."

Laura burst out laughing. "Yeah, right. Like I would threaten my own family?"

"You never know," Kristy piped up.

"Stranger things have happened," Stacey added.

"I suspected Steve, too," I confessed.

"Whaaaat?" Laura said.

"He is kind of quiet and mysterious," I explained.

"And we all heard he'd gotten kicked out of school in Arizona," Abby spoke up. "Not a good sign."

Laura shook her head with disgust. "That was *sooo* stupid. Sometimes he gets in trouble for being quiet. This teacher saw a bunch of

Steve's friends stealing brand-new instruments from the band room. It was late and almost dark, and the teacher thought she spotted Steve with them. Well, he wasn't. He was home, because he'd refused to steal. The next day, the principal called all of them including Steve to the office — and Steve didn't say a word. He didn't want to betray his friends. So he was kicked out of school with the rest of them. I mean, is that dumb or what?"

Bingo. The last part of the mystery solved. I glanced at my BSC friends. We had a lot of catching up to do in the mystery notebook.

Dad was walking our way now, looking tired. "Perhaps we should clean up."

"We'll do it!" Kristy volunteered. "You guys hang out. Relax. We can use the time to have a meeting. We have a lot to talk about."

"Suit yourself," Dad said. "I'll be waiting to take home anyone who needs a ride."

As we headed toward the lighthouse, Dad and Laura went the other way, into the remaining crowd. The BSC members were finally alone.

"Okay," Kristy said softly, "which one of you whispered, 'He's outsiiiiide' when the lights went out upstairs?"

"Not me," said Abby.

"I was too busy shaking to speak," added Stacey.

"Mallory and I were on the stairs," Mary Anne reminded us.

"I heard it, too, Kristy," exclaimed Jessi, "but I thought it was you!"

I didn't say a word. But as I entered the lighthouse, my knees were shaking.

About the Author

ANN MATTHEWS MARTIN was born on August 12, 1955. She grew up in Princeton, NJ, with her parents and her younger sister, Jane.

In addition to the Baby-sitters Club books, Ann has written many other books for children. Her favorite is *Ten Kids, No Pets* because she loves big families and she loves animals. Her favorite Baby-sitters Club book is *Kristy's Big Day*.

Ann M. Martin now lives in New York with her cats, Gussie and Woody. Her hobbies are reading, sewing, and needlework — especially making clothes for children.

THE BABY-SITTERS CLUB

Look for Mystery #28

ABBY AND THE MYSTERY BABY

I was feeling great as I turned into our U-shaped driveway. There's nothing like a good, brisk run to make you feel pumped up and happy, even in February. I'd decided I was going to nuke a bean burrito for my snack, and I was looking forward to the quiet couple of hours I'd have before my BSC meeting later that afternoon.

I trotted up the driveway, slowing my pace in order to cool down a little before my postrun stretching routine. I usually stretch on our front porch, which is humongous. As I approached, I saw a bulky, light-colored object near the front door. (It stood out because the door, which is beautifully carved, is made out of dark wood.) Was it a package? Maybe it was the new bike helmet I'd ordered. That would be excellent. But as I drew closer, I saw that it wasn't a package at all.

It was a car seat. A small, gray one. The kind

people use for babies. It was just sitting there on the porch, which I thought was weird. Why would someone leave a car seat on our front porch? Forgetting all about my stretching routine, I stepped up onto the porch to take a look.

The car seat wasn't empty.

There was a baby in it. A living, breathing, squirming baby — about four months old, to my expert baby-sitter's eye.

Someone had left a baby on our doorstep.

Read all the books
about **Claudia**
in the Baby-sitters Club series
by Ann M. Martin

THE BABY-SITTERS CLUB®

Collect 'em all!

100 (and more)
Reasons to Stay Friends Forever!

More titles... ➧

❑ MG48226-2	#82	Jessi and the Troublemaker	$3.99
❑ MG48235-1	#83	Stacey vs. the BSC	$3.50
❑ MG48228-9	#84	Dawn and the School Spirit War	$3.50
❑ MG48236-X	#85	Claudi Kishi, Live from WSTO	$3.50
❑ MG48227-0	#86	Mary Anne and Camp BSC	$3.50
❑ MG48237-8	#87	Stacey and the Bad Girls	$3.50
❑ MG22872-2	#88	Farewell, Dawn	$3.50
❑ MG22873-0	#89	Kristy and the Dirty Diapers	$3.50
❑ MG22874-9	#90	Welcome to the BSC, Abby	$3.99
❑ MG22875-1	#91	Claudia and the First Thanksgiving	$3.50
❑ MG22876-5	#92	Mallory's Christmas Wish	$3.50
❑ MG22877-3	#93	Mary Anne and the Memory Garden	$3.99
❑ MG22878-1	#94	Stacey McGill, Super Sitter	$3.99
❑ MG22879-X	#95	Kristy + Bart = ?	$3.99
❑ MG22880-3	#96	Abby's Lucky Thirteen	$3.99
❑ MG22881-1	#97	Claudia and the World's Cutest Baby	$3.99
❑ MG22882-X	#98	Dawn and Too Many Sitters	$3.99
❑ MG69205-4	#99	Stacey's Broken Heart	$3.99
❑ MG69206-2	#100	Kristy's Worst Idea	$3.99
❑ MG69207-0	#101	Claudia Kishi, Middle School Dropout	$3.99
❑ MG69208-9	#102	Mary Anne and the Little Princess	$3.99
❑ MG69209-7	#103	Happy Holidays, Jessi	$3.99
❑ MG45575-3		Logan's Story Special Edition Readers' Request	$3.25
❑ MG47118-X		Logan Bruno, Boy Baby-sitter	
		Special Edition Readers' Request	$3.50
❑ MG47756-0		Shannon's Story Special Edition	$3.50
❑ MG47686-6		The Baby-sitters Club Guide to Baby-sitting	$3.25
❑ MG47314-X		The Baby-sitters Club Trivia and Puzzle Fun Book	$2.50
❑ MG48400-1		BSC Portrait Collection: Claudia's Book	$3.50
❑ MG22864-1		BSC Portrait Collection: Dawn's Book	$3.50
❑ MG69181-3		BSC Portrait Collection: Kristy's Book	$3.99
❑ MG22865-X		BSC Portrait Collection: Mary Anne's Book	$3.99
❑ MG48399-4		BSC Portrait Collection: Stacey's Book	$3.50
❑ MG92713-2		The Complete Guide to The Baby-sitters Club	$4.95
❑ MG47151-1		The Baby-sitters Club Chain Letter	$14.95
❑ MG48295-5		The Baby-sitters Club Secret Santa	$14.95
❑ MG45074-3		The Baby-sitters Club Notebook	$2.50
❑ MG44783-1		The Baby-sitters Club Postcard Book	$4.95

Available wherever you buy books...or use this order form.
Scholastic Inc., P.O. Box 7502, 2931 E. McCarty Street, Jefferson City, MO 65102

Please send me the books I have checked above. I am enclosing $_____
(please add $2.00 to cover shipping and handling). Send check or money order–
no cash or C.O.D.s please.

Name_____ Birthdate_____

Address _____

City_____ State/Zip _____

BSC5962

THE BABY-SITTERS CLUB®

by Ann M. Martin

Collect and read these exciting BSC Super Specials, Mysteries, and Super Mysteries along with your favorite Baby-sitters Club books!

BSC Super Specials

☐ BBK44240-6	Baby-sitters on Board! Super Special #1	$3.95
☐ BBK44239-2	Baby-sitters' Summer Vacation Super Special #2	$3.95
☐ BBK43973-1	Baby-sitters' Winter Vacation Super Special #3	$3.95
☐ BBK42493-9	Baby-sitters' Island Adventure Super Special #4	$3.95
☐ BBK43575-2	California Girls! Super Special #5	$3.95
☐ BBK43576-0	New York, New York! Super Special #6	$4.50
☐ BBK44963-X	Snowbound! Super Special #7	$3.95
☐ BBK44962-X	Baby-sitters at Shadow Lake Super Special #8	$3.95
☐ BBK45661-X	Starring The Baby-sitters Club! Super Special #9	$3.95
☐ BBK45674-1	Sea City, Here We Come! Super Special #10	$3.95
☐ BBK47015-9	The Baby-sitters Remember Super Special #11	$3.95
☐ BBK48308-0	Here Come the Bridesmaids! Super Special #12	$3.95
☐ BBK22883-8	Aloha, Baby-sitters! Super Special #13	$4.50

BSC Mysteries

☐ BAI44084-5	#1 Stacey and the Missing Ring	$3.50
☐ BAI44085-3	#2 Beware Dawn!	$3.50
☐ BAI44799-8	#3 Mallory and the Ghost Cat	$3.50
☐ BAI44800-5	#4 Kristy and the Missing Child	$3.50
☐ BAI44801-3	#5 Mary Anne and the Secret in the Attic	$3.50
☐ BAI44961-3	#6 The Mystery at Claudia's House	$3.50
☐ BAI44960-5	#7 Dawn and the Disappearing Dogs	$3.50
☐ BAI44959-1	#8 Jessi and the Jewel Thieves	$3.50
☐ BAI44958-3	#9 Kristy and the Haunted Mansion	$3.50
☐ BAI45696-2	#10 Stacey and the Mystery Money	$3.50

More titles ➡

The Baby-sitters Club books continued...

❏ BAI47049-3	#11 Claudia and the Mystery at the Museum	$3.50
❏ BAI47050-7	#12 Dawn and the Surfer Ghost	$3.50
❏ BAI47051-5	#13 Mary Anne and the Library Mystery	$3.50
❏ BAI47052-3	#14 Stacey and the Mystery at the Mall	$3.50
❏ BAI47053-1	#15 Kristy and the Vampires	$3.50
❏ BAI47054-X	#16 Claudia and the Clue in the Photograph	$3.99
❏ BAI48232-7	#17 Dawn and the Halloween Mystery	$3.50
❏ BAI48233-5	#18 Stacey and the Mystery at the Empty House	$3.50
❏ BAI48234-3	#19 Kristy and the Missing Fortune	$3.50
❏ BAI48309-9	#20 Mary Anne and the Zoo Mystery	$3.50
❏ BAI48310-2	#21 Claudia and the Recipe for Danger	$3.50
❏ BAI22866-8	#22 Stacey and the Haunted Masquerade	$3.50
❏ BAI22867-6	#23 Abby and the Secret Society	$3.99
❏ BAI22868-4	#24 Mary Anne and the Silent Witness	$3.99
❏ BAI22869-2	#25 Kristy and the Middle School Vandal	$3.99
❏ BAI22870-6	#26 Dawn Schafer, Undercover Baby-sitter	$3.99

BSC Super Mysteries

❏ BAI48311-0	The Baby-sitters' Haunted House Super Mystery #1	$3.99
❏ BAI22871-4	Baby-sitters Beware Super Mystery #2	$3.99
❏ BAI69180-5	Baby-sitters' Fright Night Super Mystery #3	$4.50

Available wherever you buy books...or use this order form.

Scholastic Inc., P.O. Box 7502, 2931 East McCarty Street, Jefferson City, MO 65102-7502

Please send me the books I have checked above. I am enclosing $ _____ (please add $2.00 to cover shipping and handling). Send check or money order — no cash or C.O.D.s please.

Name_____Birthdate_____

Address _____

City_____State/Zip_____

Please allow four to six weeks for delivery. Offer good in the U.S. only. Sorry; mail orders are not available to residents of Canada. Prices subject to change.